Wylder's Jade Princess

by

Sarita Leone

The Wylder West Series

Wylder's Jade Princess

Cover Art by *Tina Lynn Stout*

The Wild Rose Press, Inc.
PO Box 708
Adams Basin, NY 14410-0708
Visit us at www.thewildrosepress.com

Publishing History
First Edition, 2024
Trade Paperback ISBN 978-1-5092-5676-1
Digital ISBN 978-1-5092-5677-8

The Wylder West Series
Published in the United States of America

Dedication

For Sharon Simpson, the strongest, kindest, wisest woman I have ever known. So blessed that she is my mother, and so grateful we are so close. I love, love, love you, Mom. Thank you for being the best, always.

And for my husband, Vito. Sempre per sempre.

Prologue

Imperial Palace, Sichuan province, China
February 1878

Candlelight danced on the ancient marble walls and golden ceiling in Queen Chen Ji's private receiving chamber. Rainbowed hues sparkled on surfaces, bringing multi-colored movement to the immense room. Beyond the flashes of light, shadowed corners. But here, within the intimate cluster of hand-carved mahogany wood seating, light.

And love.

All her life, Jiang Ying Yue had known her grandmother commanded attention from their people. She had watched the regal woman perform the obligations of their lineage with grace and wisdom, always leading her people in directions meant to keep them a thriving secure society. A place where families supported each other, as well as the ancestors who made their present situation possible. They never went without, unlike many neighboring provinces, due to the wisdom, compassion, and strength of their royal family.

China had suffered a devastating drought for two years, and there was no end in sight. The northern provinces had been especially hard hit. Crops failed, food grew scarce, people died. Many, many people.

But their home nestled in a southern province. While

people were understandably fearful of the drought spreading and impacting them the way it had done to the north, they were all safe. For now, anyway.

Her grandparents reassured those in their care, and, like a stone tossed in a still pond, the ripples of their kindness spread to touch others. Fear could be stamped out by compassion. That lesson had been one of the first she'd learned at her imperial grandmother's knee.

Jiang Ying Yue had never questioned her grandmother's decrees. She had followed the woman's instructions always, without protest.

Until this very moment.

Now, she couldn't blindly agree to the instructions she had just been given.

She wouldn't.

Jiang Ying Yue glanced over at her brother. Her eldest sibling Jiang Feng Mian's expression echoed the discomfort in her heart. Well, good. Perhaps if they protested in unison, this ridiculous proposal might vanish, the way the scent of rotting cabbage is carried away by the wind.

"Grandmother, we cannot do this." She swallowed the terror rising in her throat and forced the panic from her voice. One of her earliest lessons, to practice control in all she said and did, served her well now. A deep steadying breath, then she went on. "It is impossible for us to leave China. This is our home. We belong here." The last words were uttered with an almost harsh insistence, a manner of speaking she had never used with her grandmother before.

Her brother gasped. "Sun Lin—" Sun Lin, his nickname for her from their early childhood days. She much preferred it to the longer fussier name she had been given at birth. Now he spoke the words in supplication, but she could not back down.

Her gaze met their grandmother's with courage summoned from deep within.

No one spoke to the queen so stridently, but Sun Lin's fervor could not be contained. This matter of life or death must be resolved in a reasonable manner, even if that resolution wrought a bit of unreasonable behavior. She would apologize later. Now, she must make her point and ensure her future. In China, where she belonged.

The old woman could have been carved from a chunk of the priceless green jade that the earth offered in abundance in their land. The dark eyelashes lay like slashes of inky black writing, touching her kohl-darkened eyebrows and framing the determined dark orbs that stared straight into the flames of the fire crackling in the hearth. Despite the queen's age, her alabaster skin stretched unlined over her bones. Color had risen in her cheeks and her naturally long neck lifted her chin a tad higher, but she did not flinch at the tone of her granddaughter's words.

The queen had a nickname among the family, and now she looked every inch deserving of the endearment. Due to her regal bearing and beautifully long, graceful neck, the king had proclaimed her the Jade Swan shortly after their betrothal. While the citizens of the land knew of the moniker, no one save the closest family members dared to use it.

When she had been a small child, Lin commented to her grandmother that she, too, would like a beloved nickname. So, with as much love and affection as she had always shown her favorite grandchild, the head royal declared Lin her little Jade Princess. The name stuck, a link between two females destined to lead lives that weren't entirely their own, but of service to others.

As if echoing her protest, a log snapped in the fire, sending the flames high. Light danced across the queen's features, sending her granddaughter's heart falling into her belly. She knew that look, the one the queen chose when she contemplated lecturing about how they were called to live a life larger than the one they were born to.

She knew the speech by heart, having heard it so many times. Still, she waited, praying to the ancient ones to intercede on her behalf. Surely generations of women adhering to the rigors of their birth had to count for something. Had to offer some sort of freedom. Her debt had been paid by those who went before. She had to make her grandmother see that truth.

When the elderly woman spoke, the room turned silent. The servants standing in the shadows did not shuffle their slippered feet. No one dared breathe loudly. She and her brother sat still as stone, as they'd been taught to do when listening to royal decrees. Even the flames in the fire settled, as if it, too, knew the moment to be of extreme importance.

All stood witness to the fate of their province, and none presumed to blink while it was decided.

"You, of all my grandchildren, know I cannot falter in my promise to the people. I have been born to this life, this lineage that does not ask what I want, but demands I do what is best for those who look toward this palace for guidance." She turned her gaze from the fire to meet Lin's eyes. Firelight danced in the dark irises, but they did not hold joy. Sorrow spilled from the old woman's gaze, so strong it hurt to witness.

"We are under attack, my little Jade Princess. Your sisters have been murdered by those who would steal our fortune. Their assailants know the truth, that the only way to topple this royal line and claim its wealth is to remove us from power." She paused, then shook her head. Firelight danced on the strands of her sleek black chignon. "To remove us from the face of this earth. To send us to the ancestors. It is the only way for them to achieve their goal, by stealing our place. Do you understand what I am saying?"

A sharp shiver ran up her spine, sending a spear of icy fear to her midsection. Of course, she understood. Even without having said the word, the queen told the tale in no uncertain terms.

Murder. Those who aspired to take their place in Chinese rule were trying to murder them. The entire family, because they must if their plan were to succeed. And so far, they had eliminated all four of her sisters and one brother. The brother came as a warning, since he would not be in line to rule. Their matriarchal ruling lineage offered power to the women only, so the stabbing death of her beloved younger brother did not serve any purpose other than to let the royal family see how close their enemy had come.

"I understand, Grandmother." Lin tore her gaze from the other woman's and shot an imploring look toward her only remaining brother. He did not meet her gaze, but stared stonily ahead.

So he accepted their fate. He would do as they were told, no resistance. That showed clearly in the determined set of his features. His brows were drawn so tightly across his forehead they looked connected. She had only ever seen his countenance this serious once before, and that had been the day he discovered their brother dead in the royal gardens.

Her eyes darted to the fireplace, and for an instant she thought she saw a flash of her great-grandmother's face among the flames. Hope leaped in her chest. If the ancestor had been summoned to help, there must be a way to circumvent her grandmother's will. She blinked, hoping for more of a sign from beyond, but when she opened her eyes, the fireplace held no faces. Her imagination had toyed with her mind, sending what she desired.

She swallowed and turned back to the woman beside her. The only movement to break the other's immovable form, a flicker of compassion in the eyes.

"I understand what they are trying to do, but I know our royal forces are strong." The image of her brother's bloodied body flashed through her mind, but she pushed it aside. "I have faith in our people. They will keep us safe. And our ancestors. They are guarding us, too."

"We cannot depend on others. Others depend on us. That is the way it has always been." A sigh escaped the queen's lips. "It is bad enough that across China the land is tortured, gasping for rain that does not fall. In other provinces, mourning wails fill the air. Those who lead the suffering cannot stop what is happening. They cannot force the clouds to come or demand that water drops from the sky." She looked away, into the dancing flames. A sheen on her eyes told the story in her heart, but when she turned back and their gazes locked, all sign of sentiment had vanished. "We cannot let our people down. If our enemies claim all of us, there will be nothing left for us to offer our people. And that is what we have been born to do. Ages upon ages, women of our family have led our people. We cannot allow that to end."

She knew all of what her grandmother said was true, but she could not—would not—give up. Not yet, when she might still persuade the matriarch to relent.

"It will end if I leave. Don't you see that? If you send me away, how can I serve as queen someday? I will be a princess lost in the world, with no kingdom to rule, no one to serve."

The words caught in her throat. She did not want to leave her beloved home. China, its people, her grandmother…they were what gave her life meaning. How could anyone think sending her far from all she knew and loved could be wise?

The queen leaned over and laid a hand over Lin's folded hands. They were in her lap, nestled against the folds of her silk robe. She had been taught to sit thusly, and even now when she would like to flail her arms and scream at the injustice of the situation, her upbringing had kept her fingers at rest.

Icy fingertips covered her own. So the queen felt the chill of the situation, as well.

"If you stay, our enemies will not relent until they see us both sent to the afterworld. If you stay, they will not stop attacking us until you are murdered. I will not allow that." A squeeze from the hand surrounding her own. "I will not allow our enemies to kill my Jade Princess. You must go. Follow the directions your grandfather has in place for your escape. When it is safe for you to return, your brother will bring you home. Until then, you will stay away from China."

Defiance lifted her chin. "I w-won't." She forced the wobble from her voice. "I won't do it."

The queen straightened. Her gaze turned steely. "You will do it. I am your queen, and you are here to serve me. It is settled. You will leave before morning and travel under cloak of darkness. Our enemies will come for you, but you will be far gone. Safe, so that when we have removed those who would do us harm from the face of our land, you may return to serve our people." She gestured for the servant standing ready near the doorway. The woman came forward, her chin bowed toward her chest and her hands folded at her waist. A flick of the queen's wrist brought the servant to Lin's side. "Leave now. Every minute you remain, you are in danger."

The servant held out a hand to indicate the conversation had reached its conclusion. An invitation for the princess to stand and do her grandmother's bidding.

So there would be no tearful goodbyes. No warm embraces. No lingering kisses on the forehead. None of the niceties she had been shown her whole lifetime. Now, the queen stared into the fire, as if her granddaughter had already gone.

She stood. She had been born to serve the people of her province. And to obey the queen until her death. This order tore at her heart, but she did what was expected. She would leave. For now. But someday, in the not-too-distant future, she would return.

Neither their enemies in China nor the queen could banish her entirely.

She would not allow it.

They all knew that if every other female in their lineage fell victim to the murderous family working to push them aside, she would become something no one ever wished upon their family. A Black Pearl—named after something so elusive and valuable most believed it did not exist. But they did, and she knew that for certain because she had seen them nestled against creamy white silk in a centuries-old wooden box in her grandmother's inner sanctum.

If she were to become a Black Pearl, the embodiment everything stolen from them, it would mean every woman in the family had perished, and only she remained. She did not know how to stop that from happening, only that she could not allow it.

For now, though, she would appease her grandmother and follow her wishes. But she intended to return to her homeland and reclaim her place in the province. She didn't know how, only that she would.

She would trade her place as little Jade Princess for a while. Also, her full name would be left behind. No more Jiang Ying Yue. She did not exist. From now on, her brother's name for her would suffice. Lin she would be…until she could reclaim her place in the palace.

Chapter 1

January 23, 1881
Wylder Territory

Snow swirled beyond the schoolroom windows, pushed by a stern winter's wind. Fluffy white triangles formed in the corners of the glass as flakes piled up on the building's wooden ledges. Every few minutes the glass rattled, causing Lin to pull the edges of her shawl closer around her shoulders.

She turned away from the scene outside and surveyed the big empty room before her.

The comforting scent of cottonwood burning in the big belly stove in the center of the schoolroom filled the space. She took a deep inhale and held it. The air in China had never held this woody sweetness. Their trees were different, as was so much else, and when firewood burned, their aroma did not come close to smelling this delicious. She savored the comforting scent as she gazed at her surroundings.

Violet Bloom, Wylder's schoolteacher, had left an hour earlier. She and Thomas Harvey, the financier she'd been keeping company with for the past few years, were planning a surprise birthday dinner celebration for Alexia, Thomas' daughter. The girl grew into young womanhood and the pair wanted to do something special for her. Thomas' wife, Alexia's mother, had died a few years back, so it fell to him to bring the girl up. He did well, especially now that Violet played a role in their lives. She gave great care to consider the young lady's feelings. The dinner party had been her idea.

Lin didn't mind that her friend left early. Truth be told, they worked together seamlessly, each pitching in to get tasks in the schoolroom and chores at home done without fuss. She had lived in Violet's little lavender house a couple of blocks from the school ever since the schoolteacher had found her hiding in a utility closet years earlier. They had become a family, almost.

She looked over at the closet now and shook her head. The fact that she'd first crept into the room, alone and without any means to care for herself, still shook her to her core. When Violet found her, she had run from the men who killed her brother and were intent on murdering her, too. She'd barely spoken English, yet had managed to communicate that she ran for her life and needed help. Thankfully, her new friend had understood her plight, taken her in, and kept her safe. When the men who murdered her brother, Jiang Feng Mian, caught up with her on Christmas Eve, Violet fought with her against them, as if Lin were her own sister. Since then, they were as close as biological sisters, and lived in Violet's home without any problems.

Until now.

To be fair, the turmoil setting Lin's nerves on edge didn't come from Violet. If anything, the other woman helped calm her jitters. Had it not been for the soothing ways and level-headed advice from the other woman, she would surely be much more wobbly-kneed than she felt.

Staying behind to set the schoolroom to rights gave her time to contemplate her situation. A few minutes of quiet, the opportunity for clarity to hopefully come to her. The chores had been minimal, just a quick sweeping and wiping the blackboard clean of chalk dust. Wylder's pupils weren't disorderly, and their teacher insisted that each tidy up their own desk and the area surrounding it.

She crossed the room and leaned a hip on the big desk in the front. Its top had already been cleared of the day's chaos and lay ready for tomorrow's lessons. She paused, took another deep breath, and closed her eyes. So far, the enlightenment she wanted hadn't arrived. Maybe if she relaxed, she would know what to do.

"Jade Princess, you were born to lead our people."

She heard her grandmother's words as clearly as if they were in the same room. The sentiment had been spoken so many times during Lin's childhood that it could have been tattooed on her heart. She had always known her place in the world and her mission in life, yet it had all been swept away. Pulled out from beneath her feet with one swift tug, the way a magician tears a tablecloth off a table, leaving the delicate china unharmed.

But she'd not been left unharmed. If anything, the removal of her life's foundation caused her endless misery. Loss of family. Banishment from the only home she had ever known. Set adrift in a world she didn't understand, disguised as a man with only her remaining brother by her side. Then, losing that sibling to the bloody hands of those who would steal her birthright.

No, she had not been unscathed. Despite the situation she currently lived, one that blessed her with a safe home and many friends, she suffered. How could she ever be happy when she knew that no matter where she went or what she did, it was not the destiny she had been born to live?

She and her brother had gotten word after leaving their homeland that their grandfather had been murdered. Grandmother was gone. She stood as the only remaining link in the chain of a powerful dynasty. The Black Pearl, the last and most valued member of the family because of the blood that ran in her veins.

If she returned to China, the possibility existed that she would be killed.

But if she didn't go back, at least for a short time to try to sort out the family dynamics and ensure their people were being cared for in a way her ancestors would approve of, she would continue to suffer. A little piece of her heart died every day that she and her homeland were separated.

Yet part of her heart had been captured by Wylder. More to the point, by a certain gentleman. And he'd claimed more than just a bit of that heart. Aside from the pieces she'd left behind in China, he had the whole thing.

Lui Wei. Just the thought of his deep brown eyes and captivating smile sent a shiver up her spine.

A doctor of Chinese medicine, he had become a gemstone dealer and jeweler in this new world. After also fleeing their beloved country, although his reasons for leaving the majestic green mountains and lush rice paddies were far different from hers, he had made his way to Wylder. When she asked why he'd chosen this town above others he'd passed through, he claimed it was because the townspeople here welcomed him when others hadn't.

Discrimination against Chinese immigrants in the developing West came hard to some, and with a dear price, and Wei had experienced many instances of hateful behavior and demeaning words as he tried to find a spot conducive to creating a new life. Lin could see in his eyes, the few times they'd discussed his journey, that he had witnessed brutality to their people. Perhaps even been a victim, as well. She couldn't tell for sure, but she surmised that he had seen and felt more hatred than he would ever share with her, and she accepted that. Some secrets were meant to be kept and those who held their deepest, darkest moments close to their hearts deserved respect.

Her ancestors knew she held fast to their own mysteries. She'd take many things to the grave, so strong was her resolve to protect the family lineage.

With that in mind, she took whatever Wei offered and turned a blind eye to that which he decided to hide. And he did the same for her, something she appreciated. He knew of her royal status, and that she and her brother left China fearing for their lives, but little more. And while she trusted him with her heart, she could not open up about her family's secrets. They weren't solely hers to share, so she kept quiet. A good thing that he did not pry, for she didn't think she would ever be able to tell him the whole truth.

But she wondered how on earth she would decide how to move forward with her life when part of her heart remained in the one she'd left behind. Could a woman turn her back on the blood running in her veins?

Footsteps sounded on the schoolhouse steps. The sound of heavy stamping as if to remove snow from footwear brought her attention back to the afternoon. Her mind released China in an instant as her gaze rose to the heavy wooden door.

When it swung open, she smiled. Snow covered the

shoulders of Wei's dark blue coat. He smacked it off with gloved hands, removed his hat, and looked up. When his gaze found hers, he returned the smile, offering more in the one expression than a thousand words could convey.

The man loved her. She had no doubt of it.

But was she worthy of such a good man's devotion? Even as she walked across the large room toward him, wisps of her musing about returning to their beloved homeland hung at the perimeter of her mind.

Not the time for looking backward, not when such a good, kind man stood before her. She pulled the edges of her lips higher and pushed memories aside.

"Well, our Miss Bloom knows you well. She said I'd find you here." The man went straight to the belly stove, so she met him there. It had been banked down for the night, but the heat came from its heavy walls in waves. He tucked his gloves into his coat pockets, held his hands out, and rubbed his palms together, all the while keeping a cheerful gaze on her. "She also said I should try to get you to lock up and go home, which is exactly what I plan to do. It's getting dark out, and the snow is falling heavier than ever. You should be safe at home with Violet, doing whatever it is that you two do in the evenings."

His smile broadened. He knew very well that when she wasn't with him, she spent her evenings reading so her English language skills might improve or putting her attention to needle and thread. Her talent with embroidery had become widely known, and many of the ladies in Wylder paid her to do custom handwork for them. She embellished the ordinary as well as garments intended for intimate use. Currently she worked on a delicate array of roses and twining vines on a sheer bed jacket that would be worn on a local woman's wedding night. Lin had been putting extra care into every stitch so as to add to the couple's happiness, the way she'd been taught to do by the seamstress in the palace where she'd learned the skill.

She turned to the windows beyond the children's desks. Wei didn't lie. Dusk had long faded and nightfall had come upon them.

Her gaze returned to his. "I didn't realize it had gotten so late."

"You look as if you have been thinking ponderous thoughts." The man's intuition did not fail him. "Perhaps something you would care to discuss?"

Wei tipped his head to one side, a pose he adopted when thoughtful, one she had seen often in the time they had been keeping company. In China, he had been a doctor and with every tilt of the head or searching look in his sparkling eyes, she saw that he must have served his patients well. Not only knowledgeable, but able to intuitively see to the heart of a person, gifted not only the doctor but the ones under his care.

A fast head shake, to deny him access to her thoughts but also to clear her mind. "No. There is nothing to talk about."

She couldn't tell him she'd lost a good hour standing in one spot, contemplating whether to remain in the Wyoming Territory or return to the palace. In the past, when she had broached the subject of returning to China, he had not been silent on the idea. And his disapproval could not be swayed, no matter how many logical reasons for going back she placed before him. No, telling him what she had in mind would only lead to a disagreement. And if she did in fact depart, she wanted to go while in his favor. No sense leaving a bad feeling between them.

If she left, she wanted Wei to remember her fondly. Not curse her for being, in his mind at least, foolish.

He hadn't gotten as far as he had in the English-speaking world by taking things at face value. That examining personality trait surfaced now.

"I hear the words from your mouth and want to believe you, but the confusion in your big beautiful brown eyes tells another story." He took a step and closed the space between them. A snowflake lay on the collar of his jacket, and her fingers itched to wipe it away. He had ventured out in the cold to see her. He could have stayed in his warm shop, beside his roaring fire, but he hadn't, and it reminded her that the man had feelings that could not be dismissed.

She didn't want to hurt him, but how could she ever live with herself if she denied the calling of her homeland to her soul?

When he reached for her hand, she allowed him to take it. The solid presence and compassion sent from his fingertips as he rubbed them across her knuckles warmed her heart. "A burden shared is lighter to carry. Why don't we talk about whatever it is that has kept you standing in this empty building alone during a snowstorm?" He waved his free hand toward the corners of the room. "You must admit, it is a lonely spot for a flower to bloom."

No other man she'd met in Wylder had the same way with words that this one did. His kindness and descriptive language reminded her of home. She heard her ancestors in his words, and while they grounded her in the new land, they also pulled her back to the source of such melodious murmurings.

The pieces of her dilemma scattered to the corners of her mind, the way threads from a burlap sack torn to bits by a pack of rabid dogs were dispersed by a strong wind. No matter how she tried, pulling her thoughts together to find a cohesive, logical way out of this predicament would not come.

Lin forced her eyes from staring into the gloom beyond Wei's shoulders. She met his probing gaze and mustered a small smile. "But even the lotus rises up from the mud. Sometimes, I think, we need to remember the mud from which we emerge."

His fingertips tightened around hers. For a long moment, Wei simply searched her eyes as if he could find what she hid. "But there is no need for the lotus to return to the mud, Lin. You understand that, don't you?" His words fell hard on her heart. So, he did see beyond the wall between what she allowed him to view and that which she concealed. He might not see everything, but the way he spoke, so quietly and with such somberness, showed he knew enough. "It serves no purpose for the blooming lotus to try to return to the mud. There is no going back."

She swallowed and tipped her chin up. "Maybe not. But there is no harm in remembering what brings us into being." A gentle tug took her hand from his. The connection between them broken, she took a step back. "And the lotus cannot forget its humble beginnings. Not ever."

A glance at the pot-bellied stove, then she moved toward the pegs on the wall where her coat hung. "We should be going. Violet will worry if I'm not home soon."

Wei followed her across the large room. They dressed for the snowy walk home in silence. When he held her coat for her, she slipped her arms into the heavy fabric but did not allow him to help close it, the way she might have done had they not been dancing around an issue. They each clearly stood on opposite sides, and despite the number of times they had visited the topic, no resolution or even middle ground presented itself.

Sometimes she wished her personality didn't come with such a stubborn streak. Then again, that obstinate refusal to give up or give in had kept her alive. So really, how could she begrudge her own nature?

When Wei pulled the heavy door inward a blast of icy air swept inside. She stepped out onto the schoolhouse steps and waited while he secured the door behind them. Then when he offered his arm for support, she took it. No sense in falling in a snowbank.

A familiar dark brown horse stood waiting at the end of the walkway, her nose lowered toward the snow and the heavy woolen blanket on her wide back dusted with white. A small but sturdy covered buggy offered a protected ride home. Lin had accompanied Wei on outings to gather gemstones in the conveyance and knew it to be worthy of the inclement weather. She climbed aboard and claimed her spot on the narrow wooden seat.

The whisper of snowflakes falling and the purply darkness surrounding them made the snowy evening intimate. When the man settled beside her, it took no imagination at all to believe they were the only inhabitants of Wylder. A gentle snap of the reins urged the horse forward, the rumble of wheels a soft "shh" as they moved over the fresh snowfall.

Lin expected he would turn the buggy around and head straight to Violet's small lavender house. Within walking distance to the schoolhouse, it lay behind them. But the man let the horse continue toward the train tracks and railway depot on the far edge of town. She didn't question his actions. They had been keeping company for long enough to know that he would never hurt her. Intentionally, with his actions, anyhow. His refusal to see her side of the need to return to China did injure her, but in a subtle, concealed way, down deep where he could never see. She suspected he knew, though.

They passed the Five Star Saloon, where the melody of a rousing piano tune drifted beyond the wooden batwing doors. Light spilled from the interior over the wide front steps. Tonight, no drunken cowboys snored against the square wooden supports or sprawled in the street beyond the steps.

Wordlessly, they continued down the street. They passed one rider on horseback, but no others. Wylder had rolled in its walkways, and its citizens were huddled around their hearths.

The snow made it hard to see much beyond the horse's nose, but in the distance to the left, the glow from candles in the windows of the Social Club offered a cozy warmth. Miss Addie's ladies were well known about town, and while many of the women whose husbands frequented the establishment were reluctant to befriend them, Lin always smiled when they met. Had Violet not taken her in, she had no doubt that the profession practiced in the Social Club would have been her only means of support. The West didn't give women in her position a lot of options.

The horse turned right, almost as if it knew the way

back to the gemstone shop belonging to its owner. Behind the shop, a small building housed both beast and the buggy. Since Violet's house stood a few blocks further, she imagined the animal would be disappointed when they passed her home.

Wei still hadn't said a word, so she drew a deep breath and searched her mind for a neutral topic of conversation. Words usually came organically between them, but in this moment, she could have been seated beside a stranger.

The uncharacteristically cold demeanor didn't suit him well. And it certainly didn't do anything good for her nerves.

"Why did you choose the long way to the house?" She kept her tone light, hoping he didn't take her question as a protest. "It would have been shorter to turn the horse around."

A slow nod sent a sprinkle of snowflakes from the brim of his hat. When they had first met, he dressed in typical Chinese apparel. Black slacks, high-collared embroidered shirts, paired with sturdy boots that would protect his feet from the rocky western soil. His glistening black hair, kept in a traditional plait, tucked into the collar of his shirts.

Now, he looked more western than Chinese. The slacks replaced by denim trousers. Beautifully intricate shirt fabrics by button-down chambray. The boots were the same but showed more wear. And his hair, still tucked into his shirt. The black Stetson hat on his head concealed his features enough that had she not known his birthplace, she could have easily mistaken him for a man born on the plains or back east, in one of those cities folks talked about so much.

One of the things that had attracted her the most to the man beside her, the wash of familiarity that came over her when she looked at him, had all but been erased. Sure, he still made her heart beat quickly and could bring a flush to her body with just a look, but his appearance had changed. She wondered if, given time, more about him would shift, become someone who didn't bring a bit of their beautiful homeland to this harsh environment.

She shot a glance to the man beside her. The upper part of his face was shaded by the brim of his hat, but the muscle working near his jawline told the story. He contemplated his reply to what should be a casual question.

Well, if he couldn't easily tell her why he'd chosen the long route home to Violet's place on a snowy evening, maybe he hid other things, as well.

A needle of distrust poked at her. Did he conceal something?

Or did the prickle come from her own concealment?

Another glance, but his gaze hadn't shifted. Still focused on the sparsely populated street ahead of them, not looking toward the shops closing or already shuttered—or to her. He couldn't meet her eyes. The needle dug deeper.

"You haven't answered me." Her upbringing would keep her submissive and quiet in the presence of a male suitor, but the wagon bench wasn't a plush seat in the palace. New rules applied, so she pressed further. "And you are unusually quiet, which makes me wonder if there is something you are trying to hide, Wei."

She felt him straighten beside her. When his shoulder brushed hers, the tingle coming from his nearness came as a warning as well as attraction. In all the time they'd spent together, she had never questioned him in this way. Theirs had been a companionable relationship, without sticking points or demands for explanations.

"That sounds like the lotus accusing the fern of growing from the slurry at the riverbank." The icy tone told more than his words. She'd annoyed him, yet he wouldn't show it directly. A gentleman through and through, he let the statement show his displeasure.

She bristled. Had he forgotten who she came from? Still, further aggravating him seemed pointless, so she swallowed the frosty retort on her tongue.

"It is possible that the fern and lotus grow in peace, despite their muddy beginnings." The horse led the buggy closer to their destination. One more turn, and they would be at Violet's doorstep. Time to end this conversation without feeding the discord brewing between them. "Peace, after all, is the whole point of this lifetime, is it not?"

A cold breeze blew snowflakes against her cheeks, so she tipped her chin down and waited for the wind to let up. When it did, she glanced up at Wei. His eyes were hidden, but he could not conceal his annoyance. It had not been blown away by winter's brisk breeze.

"Is it?" A tug on the reins slowed the horse as they came into view of their destination. The horse walked so slowly, it would have been almost faster for her to get out and stride toward the house. Wei turned to face her, lines etched between his eyebrows and his lips in a thin line. "Peace? The purpose of this life is peace?"

A lump in her throat kept her from speaking, so she nodded. The disdain in his voice chilled her more than the snowy air surrounding them.

The horse came to a stop, so he dropped the reins. The animal had been so well trained that it would not move again until commanded to do so. It was, like so much else in Wei's life, perfectly ordered and predictable. That aspect of his personality aligned with hers, as she lived best when there were no unexpected disturbances. Hard to keep this western life she'd been brought to at that level, but she tried.

Wei sighed, sounding wholly tortured. "I believed us to be of one mind, Lin. In accord with our views on life…and our hopes for the future."

Her throat tightened. "I believe that, as well. You know I do."

"I'm not certain I know that right now. You say peace is the purpose of this lifetime, but I don't agree. It is important, certainly. Our ancestors have shown that a peaceful people are happy. Content. Full of spirit and productive." He removed his hat and swept a hand over his cheek. Smooth, as ever. She had never seen him unshaven, and his palm whispered over his skin so softly she leaned closer to hear the familiar comforting sound. He gave another head shake. "But I believe love is the purpose of this lifetime. Love—between man and woman, made for each other and to provide offspring to keep their ancestors happy. To keep them all, well, peaceful. Without love there can be no peace, I'm afraid."

He looked off into the distance, and while his gaze turned to the swirling snow, she wondered just what he saw in the dancing flakes. The conversation took them both to points they'd not shared before, to places in their minds and hearts that had been sheltered. Until now.

She wondered if he could hear her heart cracking,

the way she heard the touch of his hand on his face down deep in the center of her. Everything about him touched her deeply. This new wave of displeasure, especially. Maybe even more profoundly than the happy moments they'd shared, if her aching heart were any judge.

Time felt suspended. Snowflakes dropped inches from their faces, some outlined so well she discerned their frosty edges, and others a blur of white. A snort from the horse reminded her they were not alone.

In her heart, she knew that the instant she alighted from the buggy everything between her and Wei would change. Perhaps irreparably.

Still, she could not remain cocooned in the darkness while around them the world spun in a dazzling display.

Her grandmother's voice broke the quiet. In her mind, they were in the same room, not separated by death. *You know who you are. Never give anyone the power to change the convictions of your heart.*

She gathered her courage.

"Without understanding, there can be no love." Lin gathered her skirt together and stepped out of the buggy before he could get out and come around to help her. Over her shoulder, she added, "Thank you for the ride home. I am grateful that we have been friends."

The snowy ground proved slippery, and her left foot slid before she found balance. It wouldn't do to fall now and bring even more humiliation on herself. She had to make it to the house, to close the man and his obvious disapproval out.

The painted, purple front door, always so welcoming, stood only a short distance away. She quickened her steps as she heard the buggy creak. Snow muffled his footsteps, but she didn't need to hear him to

25

sense Wei right behind her.

A hand on her arm above her elbow as she strode across the wide wooden porch and reached for the door handle.

"Wait! Lin, you can't just walk away like this." His touch stopped her, but she refused to turn around. He leaned close, his voice near her ear and his breath tickling her cheek with every word. "We have been keeping company for a long time now, and I thought we were building something together."

She considered her words. She had, too, but his behavior on the ride had shown otherwise. Time to face the truth. They were not meant to be together, no matter how desperately she wished it could be so.

With her gaze pinned on the wooden door before her, she fought for composure. Surely, if she turned to face him, she would cry, and she couldn't allow it. He already made it clear her thoughts on the meaning and purpose of life were silly. No need to let him see her emotions and think her even more ridiculous.

Remember who you are.

Her grandmother's strength kept Lin's voice steady.

"I did, also. But you are right, the lotus grows from the mud and is not meant to stay beside the fern. Equanimity is essential for some, while others value different endeavors more." She owed it to the man to meet his gaze, so she took a deep breath and turned. His eyes told a story, one that wished the words that had come between them could be recalled. But though his feelings were displayed and he made no move to hide his distress, she could not falter. They had reached this point, and she would take them to its logical conclusion. "It is time for us to see that we do not belong together." When he opened his mouth to protest, she held a hand up between them. She struggled to keep it, and her voice, steady. "No, please. No argument over this. It is clear that we want different things from this lifetime. We have separate destinies, and as much as I'd hoped we would find a way to keep walking the same path, I see it is not possible. You want love and I want peace. They are not the same, Wei."

She shut her eyes and dropped her chin. The hurt in the familiar brown gaze cut her heart to shreds. Breathing hurt, as if she were being squeezed beneath the wheels of a hay wagon.

"You cannot mean this. We may have some things to work out, but you cannot say they are impossible to resolve."

He touched a fingertip to her chin and tilted her head back. She let him do it, knowing it would be the last touch she would feel from him and even if it hurt to meet his gaze, it had to be better than not feeling his skin on hers.

"I am sorry, Wei." Her words caught, but she made herself continue. It would have been so easy to fall back, but that would only bring this hard conversation to a future date. Best to get it over with. "We do not want the same things, and there is no sense in our wasting time when it is clear we have different roads to travel. Thank you for being my friend, one of my best friends here in Wylder. I will always be grateful for the happy hours we passed."

She opened the door, thankful the entry beyond was empty. Violet must be in the kitchen, probably preparing dinner. It would give her a few moments to compose herself before she had to break this news.

It didn't occur to her to not tell Violet what happened between herself and Wei. They were as sisters, and hiding anything from her did not make sense.

One final time, she met the man's gaze. "Goodbye, Wei."

The door closed softly, before he could speak. She leaned her back against the cool wood and closed her eyes. Now, the tears fell, and she made no move to stop them.

Chapter 2

Lin gazed longingly at the storage cupboard in the schoolroom. The worn wooden door fit snugly into the wall, and had she not known it was there she might not have noticed it. Which showed that those who built the schoolhouse had done an excellent job of offering the town a functional space that served its purpose without drawing attention to its details. The main focus of the room had been, at least since the first day she had been in the building, to teach the impressionable minds of Wylder and the surrounding area. When the children gathered, their lessons were of paramount importance. Everything else fell away, including closets.

But for her, that stark utilitarian alcove could hardly be called a closet. More like an open door to the safe existence she currently enjoyed.

It seemed like a lifetime ago she had hidden herself in the dark, dusty confines, looking for shelter while she considered the options for her future. There hadn't been many. In fact, her life had come to a point that she had been sure would lead her to the same cruel fate her brother had found. Or, rather, had found him.

When she and Jiang Feng Mian had been banished from China in the hope that they wouldn't be murdered by a rival family who wanted to lay claim to what was not rightfully theirs, they thought it would be better for them. Better than having their grandparents' hearts break a little more each day as they imagined the time when their cherished granddaughter would be killed solely because she possessed the prominent position on an ancient bloodline legacy. Kill her, claim the spot that her history proclaimed Lin's. Their people would protest, but not enough to overturn the disloyal thieves. Besides, once the rightful heir was dead, what did it matter?

So, they all believed the journey from their beloved homeland would be an improvement for everyone involved. For their grandparents, certainly. But also for Lin. She watched every step she made, waiting for an assassin to jump out from behind a luxurious wall of jeweled drapery or to show up in the royal palace gardens while she walked among her flowers. She often though the last impression she had of this lifetime might be the scent of night-blooming jasmine wafting from the palace gardens, taken to the next world on her last dying breath.

For her brother, too, she believed the move would prove beneficial. Life-saving, as well, for he watched over her like a hawk tied to its nest of eggs. He never went far from her side and would have died himself before seeing her harmed.

And, in the end, that's exactly what happened. Assassins hired by their rival family followed the pair, and while they tried to blend into life on the western frontier, their adversaries were like weasels in a chicken house and found them out. Mian insisted Lin dress like a man and even procured work for her at his side laying track for the railroad. For each of her strikes onto the countless metal spikes they drove, his came twice as hard, to make up for her lesser strength. They kept up with the other teams, only because he'd pushed to protect her from the others finding out she wasn't a man, but a woman.

He'd worked himself nearly to death for her, yet it didn't save them. When he died, pushing her into the dark cover of night as he held off their pursuers, part of her died, too. His final words to her had been part of a beloved Chinese children's rhyme. *Run fast, jump high, see my smile in the moon and let the wind carry you to freedom.*

She could hear him now, the words echoing in her mind as she stared at the closet door.

Run fast, jump high.

And rather than the spicy, sweet scent of night-blooming jasmine, the stench of unwashed bodies and the tar used to seal the cracks in the shanties built to house the railway workers lingered in her mind. The smell of her brother's death, because as she fled the ramshackle building where they were hiding, she knew death had found him. She only hoped it came quickly. The scream that followed the line from the nursery rhyme didn't allow her to believe his death had been painless.

She jumped when a hand touched her shoulder.

"Lin? Are you okay?"

With a shake of her head, she tore her gaze from the closet door and turned to face her friend, the woman who had saved her from the tiny closet. Violet's lavender eyes were tinged with concern. A pair of creases ran between her eyebrows.

Regret pierced Lin's heart. She had no business worrying the other woman this way. She'd been shown nothing but kindness. To repay that hospitality with concern wouldn't do. Not at all. So she pulled the edges of her lips upward and gave her head another tiny shake.

"I am fine, thank you." Beyond Violet's shoulder, the pupils all sat quietly at their desks. Reading time, one of the only hours of the school day when silence reigned supreme. She smiled wider and brought her gaze to meet the schoolteacher's. "I let myself drift into memories, that is all. Not to worry."

The other woman glanced at the closet and pursed her lips, as if she could guess what had claimed Lin's mind. She lowered her voice and leaned close. "You're thinking about the morning we met, aren't you?"

It had been a cold morning, similar to this one. Lin had spent the night standing in darkness, and nearly collapsed when Violet opened the door. The schoolteacher meant to hang her coat in the cupboard, but instead had to jump back when Lin tumbled out.

A nod. "I am." She paused to order her thoughts. Her English had gotten so much better, but she still struggled sometimes to express herself. Especially at moments like this, when she wanted to be sure the meaning of what rose from her heart and passed her lips shouldn't be misconstrued. "I am so very grateful for you. Not only for finding me and setting me free, but for...well, for everything you have done for me. I will never forget your kindness."

The other's arm went around her shoulders. Lin let herself be pulled into a fast side hug before stepping back. She had spoken the truth. Never would she forget Violet Bloom's benevolence. Not even if they became separated by thousands of miles.

"You are like a sister to me. Neither of us will forget what has passed between us. Why, we will be too busy making new memories to let the old ones escape!"

Violet's voice came soft and inviting, and Lin would

love to let herself fall into it and be surrounded by its promise. But she knew the truth. She would not stay in Wylder forever—not without first finding out what her deserting her people in China had brought about. Despite her grandparents' and her brother's wishes that she forget her roots and build a new life in safety, she could not stop thinking about her homeland. Her people. They depended on the royal family, and by fleeing, she had let them down.

Obligations, even those that brought personal danger, could not be disregarded.

But she could not tell anyone of the plan growing in her mind. Not even her dearest friend, Violet.

Lin mustered a smile and nodded. Better to feign agreement by movement rather than words. Both were misleading, but one didn't seem as much a lie as the other.

Time to change the focus of this conversation. Violet had a reputation for digging to the heart of a matter. Her pupils knew better than to attempt to conceal anything from her. Lin did, too. So she widened her smile and waved a hand toward the wide wooden bookshelf where the McGuffy readers were kept.

"I think the shelves need dusting. And I believe the readers could use some sorting." While they tried to get the children to replace materials in an orderly fashion, they were, after all, children and their idea of organized sometimes stretched abroad from what their teacher considered proper. Now, most of the books were facing spine out, but a few had been shoved beside the others with their pages toward the room rather than their spines. "It is good to do it now, while they are reading at their desks."

Violet looked over at the bookshelf and sighed. "I would very much appreciate if you did that, Lin. It seems some of our students don't know one end of a book from the other."

"As long as they learn to read what is on the pages, I can take care of the rest."

"You are a good woman, my friend. A big help and—" The other woman paused and gave her a thoughtful look. "—you will make a wonderful mother to your own children."

They had spoken many times about their hopes and dreams for the future and both women wanted children someday. They had even spent winter evenings beside the fire, sewing small garments for babes yet to be conceived.

Now, Lin wondered if those dreams would ever come true. She swallowed hard and kept her voice steady. "As will you."

When she turned and walked to the bookshelf, a shiver of something cold swept up her spine. There were no drafts in the room, the fat-bellied stove sending heat into every corner with ease. No, whatever touched her had nothing to do with Wylder, children, or the temperature.

Her grandmother would have said the icy finger that dragged up her back belonged to destiny. A sharp reminder that one could not flinch when it called…or hide from the obligations it demanded.

****

Only one place for a man to go under certain conditions. Wei didn't stop to consider any other options but headed for solace in a glass.

There were so few patrons in the Five Star Saloon

that Wei could have rolled a wagon through the hand-worn wooden batwing doors without disturbing anyone. He scanned the faces of those seated at the bar. All locals. And in the corner, a poker game. The Harvey brothers and two men he didn't recognize. No matter. If they were with Theo and Thomas, they wouldn't be the kind to object to his stopping in for a drink.

He'd had a few scuffles with drunken out-of-towners, mostly men passing through after cattle drives or ranch hands fired for misbehavior. They objected to a Chinese man setting foot into any establishment they considered their domain—even one with sticky alcohol puddles on its flooring. But he'd been in Wylder long enough and had friends and neighbors who refused to let anyone run him out of the saloon. He was grateful for those who did not allow discrimination and hate to fester in Wylder. Still, the times without any ruckus at his walking into the place were preferable to those when he had to struggle to assert himself as a man deserving basic courtesies.

He pushed the doors open and stepped inside. The smell of tobacco and woodsmoke mingled with stale beer and sour whiskey to create a mildly disturbing assault on the nose. He knew from experience the initial reek wore off quickly, so he proceeded to the bar.

The bartender strolled over, wiping the top of the scarred slab of wood with a stained rag as he came close. They exchanged nods.

"What can I get ya tonight?" The man's words dragged out slowly, as if his lips tugged every syllable from a vat of maple syrup. Sticky, they were, the kind of drawl that may have come from back east, near the Mississippi. Wei had met men from all over since his arrival in this new place, and he'd learned to pinpoint birthplaces by the first few moments of a conversation.

He could do that with those from his home country, too. As soon as Lin opened her mouth and spoke to him, he knew she came from Sichuan province. Later, when he had admitted as much to her, she confided that she had known where he'd been born, too. Some things just marked a person for life.

It pained him to remember that first conversation with her now. So long ago, a defining moment in his life. The minute he met her, he saw their future. He imagined their marrying, maybe even in a traditional Chinese ceremony or if they couldn't figure out how to make that happen, in a style more suited for their new life here in the West.

Wei dreamed of children who looked like Lin. Lots of them. Enough to keep them happy and busy. Children who would have ample opportunities in this western world for lives filled with success. Joy. Prosperity.

He pushed those thoughts aside. Bellying up to the bar had been meant as a diversion from thinking about the woman, not an excuse to linger on morose thoughts of what might have been.

"Whiskey." He rarely drank, but sure could use one now. Anything to numb the pain of losing the love of his life. "A double."

The barkeep slid a glass half filled with amber liquid across the bar with one hand and scooped up the coins Wei placed on the worn wood with the other.

A nod of thanks, then Wei raised the glass and took a swallow. Heat burned a trail down his throat and into his gut. Damn, but the stuff was nasty! He waited for the initial assault to his senses to calm before he chanced a second swallow.

Back in China, he had been a skilled physician. Nothing he had ever learned in medical school advised a body to partake of this type of beverage. He knew it did not increase health or vitality, although some cowboys made no secret of thinking that a shot or two before they headed upstairs with one of the saloon girls gave them added vigor. Wei, with his doctor's mind, knew the alcohol only numbed their senses enough that they felt stronger after the drink than they did without it.

His doctor's mind told him that his desire to numb his senses wasn't much different from the randy cowboys who did the same. The only difference, he had no interest in paying a woman to pass a few hours in one of the rumpled saloon beds with him. No, he needed to give himself a good while without a woman on his mind, in his heart, or tormenting his soul.

How the hell had he ever fallen so deeply in love with a woman? Another swallow of the whiskey in the glass he held brought the level of liquid down considerably. It also lit a fire beneath the smoldering anger living in his center. How he fell in love was less important than owning up to the fact that he had no idea how he'd pushed her away.

Didn't Lin see how much he loved her?

Apparently not, he thought as he emptied the glass and signaled for a refill. He tossed more money on the bar, nodded his thanks, and took a first swig. Not that bad, this time around. It still burned its way down and certainly it would live up to the name rotgut if he drank enough of it, but he didn't care. Let it eat his innards and light a fire in his esophagus hot enough for him to spit flames. Maybe some of the anger smoldering in him would find a release.

Because while he didn't generally let his emotions rule, and he had seen enough damage done through anger and the confrontations it brought that he didn't approve of any measure of fury in a man, he had to admit he harbored a growing rage. It grew within him, radiating from his heart and spreading, like a fire he could not control.

A small sip of whiskey, just enough to coat the inside of his mouth, as he contemplated his hostility. The sensation, so foreign as to be intriguing, offered cause for investigation. If he still lived in China, he would go to an elder and discuss his anger. The conversation would probably occur over a cup of jasmine tea. He'd ask for wisdom, which when received he would consider. Then, the path before him would appear, the way it always had whenever he found himself faced with a dilemma. But there were no elders here. If anything, he occupied that position, even though he wasn't long in years. The other Chinese men he'd seen in Wylder were workers passing through, laying track for the railroad or checking the stakes on existing rails. They never lingered and if they had, Wei would be considered the wise elder among them.

So he had no one to turn to. Except…

He held the glass up toward the light. The wicks in the candles in the closest chandelier offered light through grimy, smoky glass globes, but they shone brightly enough that the amber liquid almost glowed. Magic in a glass.

Many of the men he'd become friendly with sometimes sought the answer to their problems at the bottom of a whiskey bottle. They were good people, not no-account drunks. They weren't passed out on the saloon's front walkway or tumbling down its wooden steps into the street.

He had never believed it possible to learn anything from drinking alcohol, but perhaps he'd been wrong. After all, nearly every man in Wylder, with the exception of the Catholic priest and the minister whose name he didn't know, drank. And none of them staggered home. Not that he knew of, anyhow.

He brought the glass to his lips and tipped his head back. Funny thing about drinking…the more he did it, the easier it got. The glass made a dull thud on the counter as he set it down. As he dug in his trouser pocket for more money, a hand touched his shoulder.

"This one's on me." Theo Harvey placed his own empty glass on the counter and nodded to the barkeep. "Fill 'em up, please." He slid onto the worn stool next to Wei's and cleared his throat. "Don't see much of you in here, Wei. Special occasion?"

Theodore Harvey had a homestead just outside of town where he lived with his wife, Lily, and their young child. At the moment, it didn't come to Wei whether the child was a boy or girl, but that didn't matter. A child was a child, a blessing to any family.

The Harveys came to town a few times a week, a fact Wei knew from their business dealings. Missus Harvey came to his shop for unctures and ointments for scratches and other minor skin problems.

Last fall she had gotten into some poison ivy while clearing for an extension to her vegetable garden. Fortunately, he had enough herbs and roots in his supply cupboard to concoct a paste to minimize the pain and reduce the chance her creamy skin would be scarred. The paste worked, and she had told the other women in town that he'd saved her when she'd been in a bad way. As a result, he regularly sold that paste as well as several other ointments to local women. Ironic that in this new frontier lifestyle, the ways of ancient traditional Chinese medicine were widely used. He wished his teachers at his old medical school could see this minor remedial miracle.

But they couldn't. Like all that he had left behind, they were part of his past and while he longed sometimes for the old ways, he had made a serious attempt to fit in with these different western ways. Progress meant not going backward, which came as the sticking point between him and Lin.

"You certainly are eyeball deep in your own thoughts." Theo nudged Wei's elbow with his own. They were both leaning onto the bar top, their arms separated by a few inches. "Don't even see the refill, do you?"

He realized he'd been miles from the saloon. A shake of his head to clear his mind, but it only chased half the cobwebs from between his ears. A good deal of fuzziness remained, but he let himself rest against the softness in his head. Such a nice distraction from the heat and anger brewing in the rest of him...

"Wei? Are you okay?" A second elbow nudge, this time more forceful than the last.

Hell, he'd best get himself together before someone called for the doctor. The last thing he needed, for Coyote to see him half drunk and with a wandering mind.

"I'm fine." He took a slug of the whiskey and waved the glass between them. "Thanks for the drink. Next one's on me."

"Well, now, I'm not so sure we need to be drinking

much more." The other man closed one eye and swept his gaze over him. "Looks to me like you already drank more than I ever seen you do. Lookin' a mite fuzzy around the edges, my friend."

Fuzzy. The exact way he felt. Funny that his outside matched the inside.

A chuckle chased away some of the anger still coursing through him. "Fuzzy...I must agree on that point. That about sums it up, at least the part above my neck."

Theo swallowed the liquid in his mouth and let out a long, slow exhale. The scent of whiskey washed over both of them. It no longer hit Wei the way it had when he walked into the saloon an hour—or was it two?—ago. The liquored-up air between them welcomed him and he inhaled its sweet aroma.

"And the rest of you?"

The rest of him? Should he admit to the intensity of these foreign feelings?

Whiskey. Maybe it was the courage in a bottle he'd heard it called, because he took another long swallow of the alcohol in his glass before slapping his other hand on the worn wooden bar so hard it stung.

He turned to Theo and locked his gaze on the other's kind eyes. If he were going to confide in anyone, this man offered a fine spot to do so. He couldn't be sure his friend wouldn't be shocked by his admission, but he had to tell someone.

"The rest of me is as riled up as a rooster in an abandoned henhouse." Yes, that was about right. He scrubbed a hand over his chin. "Lost. Lonely."

The other cleared his throat. "Well, there's always the girls over at the Social Club. Y' know Miss Addie ain't never been a discriminating woman. Every man, long as he's decent with her girls, is welcome. You could get your, ah, loneliness worked out for sure over there." He paused to take a drink, then shook his head. "Not that I'm spendin' my time or silver over there, mind you. I'm a married man, and I take my vows seriously. But I haven't always been hitched, you know. Wasn't that long ago I was feelin', ah, lonely now and again. Miss Addie's gals, well, they make a man feel loved in two twitches of a coyote's nose." He grinned. "Believe me, you won't be feelin' lost anymore after a spell between the sheets."

The Wylder County Social Club, just the opposite side of the railroad tracks, had kept many men from feeling lonely. Miss Addie and her girls were held in high regard by both men and women alike. Wylder's ladies welcomed them to social events, knowing full well the madam and her women would get gussied up and contribute nicely to whatever fundraiser or potluck supper they held. There were very few who didn't recognize those from the whorehouse as vital members of their small community.

Wei had never crossed the madam's threshold. Sure, he nodded a greeting to the women when he passed them on the street, and while he didn't know each girl's name, he recognized them by sight. They were all pretty and smiled at everyone as they went about their business.

But he had never availed himself of the services they offered.

Maybe he should consider stepping in, just to see how it felt. Like trying on a new pair of boots, a man had to put his feet into them to know if they'd be a good fit or not. He had no experience with Miss Addie's kind of woman, but he didn't imagine it would be too hard to get used to having a warm body beside him. And the girls at the club were pretty as shiny new silver dollars, besides. No man in his right mind would turn down a spell with any of them.

Something tugged on his heartstrings and pushed its way into his conscience. He loved Lin. Wasn't any way to stay true to his heart, thinking about straying into another woman's bed, was it?

But hadn't he waited patiently for Lin to welcome him to her bed? He'd courted her all right and proper-like, done everything he could to show how highly he regarded her and how much he hoped to build a future with her. Heck, he'd even come right out and said as much, hadn't he?

Another swallow of whiskey did little to remove the sour taste of bile that rose in his throat. His heart might be saying one thing, but his gut surely had other words to share.

He had offered the woman all he had, and she'd turned him down. The words ringing in his head left no room for doubt—she'd broken things off with him without even shedding a tear over it. He'd been tossed aside like a used…well, like something of no value at all.

A second swallow and the bitter taste on his tongue cleared a bit.

Lin didn't want him, and no matter how much that hurt, it was a fact. Plain and simple, no room for misconstruing her intention.

He turned to Theo and gave a hard nod. "I'm thinkin' you just might have a point. About Miss Addie's girls, that is." He drained his glass and set it down on the bar with enough force his wrist tingled. But when a man made up his mind over something, it didn't do to be all wishy-washy about it, did it? Certainly not. He reached for his hat and slapped it onto his head. "I'm goin' over there right now and see w-what's available."

His mouth felt filled with cotton and he contemplated ordering another drink to wash the fuzziness away, but time didn't stop for drinking, and he had some real feelings to have swept away. If one woman wouldn't love him, he'd find another who would—even if he had to pay her.

Theo put a hand on his shoulder, so Wei paused halfway up off the barstool. His behind hung in the air and his legs wobbled, but he found his balance.

"Are you sure you should be goin' anywhere tonight? My friend, you ain't lookin' your best." He tipped his head, then shook it. "Fact is, you're lookin' like you couldn't hit the ground with your hat in three tries!"

Concern showed in the other man's eyes, but Wei shook his head and forced a smile. He pushed against the bar and stood.

"No w-worries. I'm fine. Jus' a little bit tired, is all." He reached for his hat, then remembered it already sat on his head. His hand dropped to his side, so he let it hang. Darn, but his fingers felt tingly! "An' it's been a long time coming, this tired. I wasted a lot hopin' and wishin' for something that wasn't meant to happen. Now it's time to…time to…"

Time to what? Damned if he could remember, exactly.

So he smiled wider and turned toward the door. He'd waited long enough to begin his life. Damned if he'd put it off another minute. If Lin didn't want him…well, he'd find his pleasure elsewhere. And while none of Miss Addie's ladies were going to leave their chosen life to run off with an ordinary Chinese doctor-turned-gem dealer, he might find someone who would think him appealing. In time, that was. For now, the Social Club would be enough.

One last grin to his friend as his palm hit the cold wooden batwing and pushed the door open. "It's just time, is all."

Chapter 3

Every item laid out on the embroidered quilt meant something to her, but she would have to leave some of them behind. Lin planned to travel as lightly as possible, which meant only absolute necessities could be considered for packing. Still, the things spread before her on the delicate ivory fabric were all special. Each had meaning, and as her gaze traveled over them her heart warmed.

It hit her that everything she valued, all the possessions she had gathered, had come to her after she arrived in Wylder. Along with all the beautiful memories she had from the past three years, she treasured this small collection of material goods. They represented so much, yet were still meager.

When she and her brother left China, they didn't take much of anything. The clothes on their backs, two small rucksacks containing some food for the journey, and funds for their passage. A vicious change, to go from the palatial opulence they had been born into, to moving like paupers to a new land. They had been on the same level as the rats scurrying about in the bowels of the enormous ship they'd booked passage on. Hiding from the light and trying to survive at any costs, willing to do whatever it took to evade those who would not hesitate to take their lives, even if it meant concealment in horrible places and taking risks that were mind-numbingly frightening. Anything to stay alive.

They had managed to keep from being killed, which was more than she could say for most of the vermin on the ship. Desperation drove many packed tightly into the lower decks to search for food and to the hungry, meat of any sort filled the empty corners of their bellies. She and her brother had not resorted to trapping and preparing the ship's vermin, but had witnessed others doing so. She could not blame them. Anything to survive. And many had small children to care for and would do whatever it took to keep the hungry wails silenced.

So much suffering.

Many who attempted the crossing did not finish with their lives. Countless bodies claimed by the sea, gone before land came into sight. Lost to the journey, silenced with their unrealized hopes and dreams.

Sadness and resignation married hunger for passengers left in the hold. She and her brother huddled together, praying they wouldn't be touched by any of it. And as others perished, they were all afforded more room in the miserable belly of the ship. Fewer who took up space or breathed the foul, stinking air. Not as many to fill the slop buckets or vomit in the night.

The horrors of the journey were behind her, yet they were still too clear in her memory for comfort. They were unforgettable harsh moments in time that were able to bring her nightmares, even now.

A shudder jolted her as she tucked the memories aside. That wouldn't happen again, not with this crossing. Her passage wouldn't be as awful. It couldn't be. She had money put aside and planned to purchase passage anywhere in the ship but the lower deck. A

Chinese woman traveling solo could never imagine she could find safety in one of the better cabins, but if she could secure space in a female passenger communal cabin, she would take it. Anything to not be in the dark with the rats again. Whatever it took, she would pay to avoid another nightmarish journey.

This time, she would be alone.

No brother to protect her or hide her face against his shoulder, so she didn't see the worst of the horror.

No one to shield her from leering glances from fellow passengers.

No chance to pass the hours reminiscing over their childhood or sharing dreams of what lay before them.

No one to care whether she reached China alive or slipped into the murky seawater and be claimed by the ocean, just another unmarked death.

Lin shook her head to clear it. She couldn't ruminate over what couldn't be changed or overthink the arduous journey ahead of her. If she did, she might wail over the grievous past or lose her courage to face the future.

And that would be failure, something she couldn't allow. Her grandmother had been wrong to send them away. She realized it had been done out of love, and a hope to keep a Jade Princess alive, but her place had been with her family. They were gone now, and aside from remote cousins, there would be no one to care for their people. Generations of sacrifice and nobility, all wasted.

She hoped one of the distant relatives had stepped up and taken the lead left by her grandparents' passing, but hoping and knowing were two different things. If a cousin had taken the role and burden, and the families who looked to their lineage were being cared for, Lin didn't necessarily have to remain in China. She could step back, which she of course hoped remained a possibility. It would be a great relief to not have to shoulder the weight, and be able to choose her own path in life.

But if no one led, and the people suffered, she would stay.

And if the people were doing well, safe and satisfied, she would…

She would what? That question niggled her constantly, but she had gotten very good at pushing it aside. How could she cross one bridge without first seeing if it wasn't just a wish rather than a reality? And she could not discount the thought that the way back wasn't always open to those who went forward. If she left Wylder, and Wei and the beloved Bloom sisters, they might not welcome her back should she decide to return.

All so much on her mind and heart. She hadn't gotten to China, and the weight already crushed her. How on earth would she manage to fulfill the destiny she had been born to? And how to know if one's destiny could change, become fluid as a result of the situations surrounding one? They were all ripples in a pond, each having an impact on the next, each able to change the ripples nearest them. She had learned this as a child, that no one tiny wave ever remained alone and unaffected by others. The philosophy had brought her to this point, but would it bring her further in life?

Too much to ponder and too many questions. They all made her head ache.

The sound of a door opening, then closing, from the front of the house grabbed her attention. It pulled her from the whirlpool of emotions and thoughts that moved so swiftly within her that she almost felt physically ill.

The tapping of heels against hardwood flooring came closer, so she hurried to the bedroom door and went through to the hallway, closing the wooden slab behind her. Violet would not pry, so while it wasn't usual for the door to be shut, she wouldn't be questioned.

As she had thought, the other woman headed straight toward her.

"Oh, Lin, I'm glad you're home. It was so quiet when I came in, I wondered if you were napping." Violet tipped her head toward the door. "I thought to check in on you and not disturb you if you were sleeping."

A fast wipe of a suddenly clammy hand down the front of her dress as she searched to arrange her features into a bland—and she hoped, innocent—expression. She shook her head with a small smile. "No, not sleeping. Just resting."

No one would have guessed the woman smiling at her with a look of concern in her eyes had just been in a schoolroom with three dozen children since just past sunrise. Not a hair had come undone from the other's upsweep and her blouse and skirt were as wrinkle-free as they had been when she set out so many hours before.

Now, as they walked into the kitchen, a lump formed in Lin's throat. She had never had a friend as wonderful as Violet before and didn't think she would ever find another nearly as good-hearted and kind. She hated leaving her behind, but couldn't put off her own destiny any longer. No, tomorrow she would set off for her homeland. Once the schoolteacher left the house, she planned to leave, too.

So tonight would be their last evening together. She wished there was some way to express how much this time in Wylder meant to her, but she couldn't risk having

Violet try to dissuade her from going.

Lin swallowed hard, blinking and pushing the tears that sat ready to fall down her cheeks back into her eyes. Time enough to cry later. Now, to make the most of what they had left.

She gestured to the nearest chair, the one that her friend favored. A needlepoint pillow softened its hard back. The purple irises worked on its fabric were a bit flattened from long hours spent supporting a weary back, but were still pretty enough to call a summer garden to mind.

"You've worked hard with the children all day. Let me get you a cup of tea, then I'll begin dinner."

A grateful sigh escaped the other's lips as she settled on the wide wooden seat. "That sounds lovely. And just so you're entertained while you cook, I'll tell you a story about a little boy, a very small piglet, and a Stetson that will never be the same again…"

****

Wei added an extra pinch of ground kudzu leaf to the mixture in the ancient stone mortar. He had made the traditional Chinese hangover remedy many times for others, but never for himself. Until now. He ground the ingredients together with the pestle, wincing at the soft grinding sound that accompanied his pulverizing the assorted herbs.

It made no sense that men would inflict this kind of agony on themselves, but he knew they did. Establishments like the Five Star Saloon were common on the western frontier. And in other areas, taverns thrived, as well. He'd witnessed drunkenness in every place he'd been but had never thought much about it. Certainly, undignified behavior ensued when alcohol was consumed, but he wasn't judgmental. Let others do as they pleased, as long as it hurt no one.

Well, his throbbing temples were proof that imbibing did harm. So much so that the very thought of whiskey sent his gut topsy turvy and his head near to exploding. What possessed a man to do such harm to his own body? What had he been thinking?

Enough. He couldn't stand one more second of scraping from within the small container. He tipped the contents into the pot of water he'd boiled, set the lid in place, and waited. A few minutes with the herbs, and the concoction would be ready for drinking. Then, as soon as his head cleared, he planned to search out Lin.

They had to clear the mess between them.

He'd nearly done something deplorable last night. Again, he never judged others, but he had no mind for sleeping with a woman who did not have a place in his heart. Miss Addie's lady had been very sweet and accommodating, but he could not bring himself to have relations with her. He'd refused her friendliness and the offer of a beverage. Instead, he had fallen asleep in the woman's bed fully clothed—and had been relieved he'd woken the same way.

After depositing a generous stack of silver coins on the bedside table, he'd made a quick exit from the place. The hallways had been empty, no one in sight to witness his leaving. The walls had eyes, though. One could never be entirely certain that they had not been observed. But he had hope that no one had seen him leave in the early hours.

And if he was lucky, the brew sending stomach-turning fumes into the air now would let him get rid of the worst of his hangover before anyone witnessed that, as well. He poured a measure into the cup he favored, put the rest back onto the table, and raised the cup to his lips.

His belly protested, but he swallowed, then sucked in a big breath. Hot, tasting of forest and spice, the liquid burned his tongue and slid down his throat in a harsh wave. Punishment, he thought, for his undignified behavior the previous night. At home in China, he had been a physician. Here, in Wylder, he had behaved like a common drunken ranch hand.

It could not happen again. He took another mouthful and swallowed and vowed that the events of the past hours were a turning point rather than a path to follow.

Every man must be allowed to stumble, and even fall, from the path he knew took him toward his destiny. That's what had happened to him. Just a misdirected step, nothing more. And now that he had found his senses, and reclaimed his mind, his feet were back on the correct path. They had to be.

Lin. The image of her beautiful face filled his mind. His chest tightened and his knees wobbled a bit. The woman sent his whole body into fits of emotion and sensations like none before ever had. It was as if she held the key to his heart, and now that she had unlocked it, he couldn't live without her.

When he'd been a young man, his beloved grandfather had told him that someday he would meet a woman who would make him feel more than he could begin to imagine. He'd loved his grandfather, but he hadn't believed him.

The elderly storyteller also wove fantastical tales of red and blue flying dragons, warriors who leapt high stone walls on a breath, and trees that could tell the future. He had been full of wisdom, and also the type of nonsense that kept a little boy's imagination filled. As he grew, the stories required less suspension of belief, but still they came. Women replaced dragons. Good-hearted men stood in for wall-jumping warriors. And the oracles came from within, rather than from nature.

Years passed, and he still loved his grandfather, even though he knew better than to believe every word that came from the wise man's mouth.

But the old man had spoken the truth about the woman who would come into his life and touch his soul. And now Wei sat trapped by his feelings, the yearning of his heart.

He had to convince Lin that they had a future together. A good one, a destined lifetime of love and laughter. Somehow, he had to make her believe what he knew in his heart—in his soul—to be true.

Wei tipped the cup and finished the brew. It had no effect on his hangover yet, but he believed it would help. And when it did, he planned to confront Lin and do whatever he had to do to get her to be his wife. That was the only suitable option. He would convince her of such, and they would live a long happy prosperous life together. He would not entertain any other outcome.

****

Violet used the heavy leather gloves beside the big belly stove to pick up and place two lengths of wood in the fire. The wood had seasoned well, and the cottonwood caught fire instantly. She gave the upper log a jab with the long iron poker, then, satisfied that the fire would keep the schoolroom warm, closed the heavy cast iron door on the flames and removed the gloves. She placed them alongside the poker, brushed a hand down the apron she wore over her skirt, and turned to face the

54

rows of desks in the large room.

Despite the cold snowy day, her classroom was full. Pupils bent over their desks, without one empty space among them. It warmed her heart to see their noses in books and concentrated expressions on their faces. The McGuffy readers held the interest of even the older students, and for that she was thankful. Their being so occupied gave her a few minutes to attend to other things, such as keeping the fire going and writing the next batch of spelling words on the blackboard.

She crossed the room, glancing at the children as she passed them. Only one looked up from the pages of the book open before her. A small smile passed between herself and the young lady before the other's head tipped back down, and reading began again. It came as a heart warmer to have Thomas Harvey's daughter, Alexia, in her classroom. She and Thomas, a widower, had been keeping company for a number of years now, and she had grown attached to the motherless child.

At the blackboard, she reached for the length of white chalk that always sat beside the blackboard eraser. The eraser had come with her from back east, a special order from a store owned by John Hammett, the wise man who invented the tool. The children knew better than to touch either the chalk or eraser, given that replacing the one would be costly and the wait for its arrival from one of Mister Hammett's stores long.

Now she wrote the vocabulary words, taking care to keep the letters straight. Shorter words at the top of the list for the younger readers, and longer ones at the bottom for the more advanced pupils. Spelling lessons were one of her favorite parts of the day. Learning letters and reading made opportunities possible that nonreaders weren't privy to, and if she wanted anything for the children who filled her schoolhouse, it was their chance for a good future.

Without children of her own yet, these youngsters were almost as dear to her as the ones she hoped to have someday. Her beloved mother had stepped in to fill the void in several orphans' lives back home, so she had learned at an early age that a woman could provide love and guidance to all children, not just those she had birthed.

With the idea of making the lesson a bit more challenging, she added three words to the list. They were ones that wouldn't come easily to any of the children, but if they did take some time and gave it a bit of thought, they might be successful. The bottom drawer of her desk held small gifts for lessons like this one, where answers weren't apparent and those who worked a tad harder got a reward for their effort.

Violet glanced at the clock. Ten minutes more to reading time. Then, a break for lunch. She had baked oatmeal cookies the night before and would hand them out to each child. Some of her pupils arrived to school with meager offerings in their lunch sacks, so she always found a way to slip those children an extra cookie.

A hand went up near the front of the room. One of the younger pupils, Lloyd Tolbert. He came from one of the more affluent families in Wylder, and his round little body showed there was no food scarcity in the Tolbert home.

"Yes, Lloyd?"

The boy had a grin as wide as his middle. He used it now, along with a twinkle in his brown eyes that showed he hoped to charm her.

"Miss Bloom, is it lunchtime yet?" He ran a hand over his belly and shook his head so hard a brown curl fell over one eye. "I'm powerful hungry."

She resisted the urge to smile. Instead, her teacher's voice answered, "Very hungry. Or even quite hungry. But 'powerful' is not a way to describe hunger, Lloyd."

The child pulled his brows together so tightly they looked like a fuzzy caterpillar marching across his forehead, which only made it still more difficult to keep a straight face. She knew the rest of the class watched, and giving them a reason to dissolve into fits of giggles would surely rob them of their last few minutes of reading study. And that, with its opening of doors for fine futures, couldn't happen.

"Well, ma'am, then I'm very quite hungry." He smiled sweetly. "Is it time for lunch now?"

A couple of the older pupils snickered at the reply, so she shot a stern look toward the back of the room before turning her attention on the persistent questioner.

"It's either 'very' or 'quite' when speaking, not both."

Another eyebrow caterpillar. "Then I'm very hungry and quite hungry, too."

She decided to accept that compromise. "Better word choices, thank you. Remember, 'powerful' is a word that describes a physical...oh, never mind. Just don't use it to describe hunger is all." A look at the watch on her wrist. The conversation had eaten up two minutes from their reading time, so she recalculated in her head before she met the waiting child's gaze. "And it is not quite lunchtime yet, so keep your mind on your reader for a few more minutes."

A long sigh from the boy, but he turned dutifully in

his seat and dropped his gaze to the open book before him.

Glad for the last quiet moments, Violet crossed to the window and looked out. Snow swirled, blown by cold gusts fierce enough to rattle the panes of glass. A gray sky, with angry clouds hanging low. Threatening. Definitely a day for folks to remain indoors if possible. A thought most of Wylder shared, apparently, since the street in front of the school stood nearly deserted. One wagon left tracks in the snow, and a man headed for the corner with his hat pulled low over his face.

Good, she thought. Best to stay out of the weather, keep from falling in snowbanks.

That's how she had met Thomas. He had rescued her from a snowbank early one snowy morning and taken her to his home when she was nearly frozen.

That's where her true life in Wylder had begun. In a snowstorm. Then inside Thomas' home. He had called for the doctor to see to her, then insisted she stay in place until she grew stronger. He'd pulled her from the snow and somehow claimed her heart, all in the matter of a few days' time.

After she returned to the schoolhouse, just in time to host the annual holiday show and party, her role in the community had changed. It was as if being dedicated enough to trudge to the schoolhouse in the wee hours during a storm, she had showed her commitment to the town and its children. Where she had felt like an outsider, suddenly she experienced a welcome unlike the one she had received when she had first arrived in Wylder.

Now, she could not imagine living anywhere else. Wylder had given her the life she dreamed of for herself, one where neighbors were friends and folks looked out for each other. Certainly, the place had its rough edges and wild moments, but didn't everywhere west of the Mississippi River have those? This wasn't the genteel streets of the South where she'd been raised. This new exciting frontier should have surprises.

And the children in Wylder and from the surrounding homesteads and ranches were dear to her. She would never trade this life for anything else.

It was a bonus that all three of her beloved sisters had followed her to the frontier. Lily and Daisy had come first, and they were so close, her life nearly felt complete. But she kept hope alive that they might manage to get Pansy, the youngest Bloom sister, to Wylder, too. Quite unexpectedly, she had shown up, and now all four sisters enjoyed their new lives. They were together again, the way she had always hoped they would be.

A smile lifted the edges of her lips high. She began to turn back to the pupils with the intention of releasing them from their studies so they could eat lunch, when a figure beyond the window pane caught her attention.

A woman. Slight build, bundled in a long coat dusted with snow. Head angled toward the ground, a scarf pulled tightly around her neck by one hand while the other clasped a small traveling bag to her chest.

The shiver that slid up Violet's spine was not pleasant. She was sure she recognized the woman, but at the same time hoped the snowstorm distorted her vision. Because if she was correct, a woman who she loved like a sister, one who should be safely home in their little lavender house a few streets away, was out in the storm. And the figure trudged through the snow as if she had a destination in mind. The snow swallowed her view, hiding her from sight and bringing a clammy sheen to

Violet's brow.

She turned from the window, crossed her arms over her chest, and tried to swallow. Her mouth had grown dry. Not one to often give fear purchase in her mind, she allowed the emotion in now simply because she could not keep it from her thoughts.

Where on earth could Lin be headed on such a dismal day? And why hadn't she mentioned her intention to leave the house this morning when the two of them had last spoken?

It didn't bode well, this snowy outing. Lin did not appreciate bad weather except from behind a pane of glass and standing beside a fire, so something important must have coaxed her from the house. But what?

****

Snow covered Lin's scarf and found its way down the back of her coat, but she didn't let that deter her from her journey. No, she wouldn't turn back now, not after it had been so hard to leave.

Had anyone told her when she arrived in Wylder with her brother and had worked alongside him disguised as a young man that she would come to consider the frontier town her home, she would have thought they were crazy. Their arrival had been marked by turmoil and fear that they were being followed. The constant worry that their identities would be discovered never left their thoughts. And, to add to it all, Lin could barely take a free breath, worried as she was that her gender would somehow be revealed. One wrong move or misspoken word, or even a badly timed change of clothing would lead to disaster.

Wylder had been a stopping point on their mad dash for their lives. Her brother believed their joining up with a Chinese work crew to service the Union Pacific Railway lines would offer concealment. Neither of them had ever done manual labor before, but they persevered, one working hard for the other to remain safe and the other doing the same. She knew that if their deception became clear, no good would come to her brother, either. His life had been tied to hers from the moment she'd been born.

And his life had ended because of her, a truth that she would never forget and forever regret. But there were things in this lifetime that could not be changed, no matter how desperately one wanted to do so, so she reconciled herself to that fact.

Never had she thought that Wylder would become home. And not just a place to settle on a transient basis, but a spot to put down roots. Find a family with the Bloom sisters and the kind citizens of the rough-and-tumble town. But that's exactly what happened.

And now an ache filled her chest at the reality that this home, this place that sheltered her and offered so much joy, would become only a memory.

You have no choice, she thought. If she had, she wouldn't be walking through the snow wishing she could turn around and return home to the lavender house.

A shoulder shrug mashed the snowflakes against the woolen fabric, making a wet spot that would probably become bigger and more miserable in time, but she didn't care about that, either. Wasn't it one of the parting words of wisdom bestowed upon her by her beloved grandmother, that one should not be deterred from one's destiny for any reason? No physical or mental challenges were daunting enough to sway one from the path. She remembered the words, and even heard the other's voice in her mind.

Well, Lin hadn't forgotten, and while she had been forced to believe her destiny waited in this foreign land, that had been wrong. She knew better now.

Another swirl of snow and a new clump of flakes made its way down her neck. A hard shrug crushed the snow, making the wet spot on the inside of her coat bigger. Like the cold splotch, her resolve grew.

Her fate waited in her homeland. And one way or another, she would make her way back. Check on her people. Lead if necessary. Assist wherever possible. But she would not remain in this new place like a scared mouse who had jumped from a chaotic ship into the safety of the ocean. She would not ride this slice of wood forever, as if this new land could keep her from her true purpose in this lifetime.

The snow lay piled beside the wooden steps leading up to the wide platform at the train depot. Someone had shoveled, thankfully. Taking care not to slip and fall, she made her way up the steps. When she reached the top, she stamped her feet to divest her boots of as much snow as possible. No need to track it inside, where someone would need to mop up the mess. No, she'd take care of her own messes, the way she always had.

A deep breath for courage, then she pushed the heavy door open and stepped inside the building. A welcome wave of heat, courtesy of the large cast iron belly stove that roared in the far corner, washed over her face. For a long moment, she stood on the thick jute rug and savored the sensation of being surrounded by heat. Her shoulders fell a bit as her joints loosened, the icy tension of making her way to this point thawing her from the outside in. At the back of her neck, the cold, wet fabric, but it hardly mattered now. Glorious heat brought strength to the points where she'd wobbled.

Amazing, what a difference a smallish change could bring. Shelter. Warmth. Things many took for granted, the niceties that made one feel nurtured and safe.

From childhood, she had been taught that one does have an obligation to make the most of this time on earth. She believed that to be true. However, she no longer thought anyone should decide for her where her obligations lay. That fell onto her shoulders, and hers alone. And now that she realized the fact, nothing would stand between her and what she knew she had to do.

Nothing.

Not even the puzzled look on the face of the man behind the ticket window. Thankfully, the inside of the train depot sheltered only the two of them. She supposed no one else was foolhardy enough to travel on such a miserable afternoon.

She took a deep breath and searched her mind for the man's name, but it eluded her. No matter. Surely this would be the final time their paths crossed.

A shake of her shoulders to send the last of the snowflakes from her coat to the planks at her feet. And another strong breath as she raised those shoulders and pulled them back, straightening her spine and hoping she looked formidable rather than the way she felt. Her insides quivered, but her lips turned up ever so slightly at the corners. Thank goodness her face worked on its own, because her mind still swirled.

The man behind the window didn't help her nerves one bit. He stared silently and waited for her to begin.

So, she began. If she was going to get back to China, she would have to deal with pinched-face glares from very obviously disapproving men. She had known that, yet this reality still turned her knees to jelly.

"I would like to purchase a railway ticket, please." Thanks to Violet's tutelage, her English language skills came with ease. She forced herself to speak slowly and enunciate every word. Her reticule hung from her wrist, so she reached for it to untie the ribbons holding it closed. "How much will that be?"

The ticket man didn't answer right away. Instead, he narrowed his eyes and huffed.

Just when she thought he wasn't going to reply, he spoke.

"You travelin' alone?" His tone was not friendly.

She swallowed hard. Solo female travelers were often frowned upon. A simple matter to move about with a husband or family, but much more challenging for a woman to do so on her own.

A look over her shoulder showed no one standing behind her, so his question came as a shock. The only other person in the depot, a man in a long black duster who had a black hat pulled so low over his face she couldn't see his features. He leaned against the wall closest to the tracks, near a window. If his shoulders hadn't moved, she might have thought him a statue, he stood so still. She hadn't seen him when she entered, but she noticed him now.

Her attention returned to the ticket man. He, too, remained so still that, paired with the other fellow, they could have been museum exhibits. That is, if museums had offerings of this size. She couldn't know for sure if that was the case since the only art gallery she had ever experienced was inside the family compound back in her homeland. There, relics of her ancestors sat side by side with precious carvings, paintings, and statues belonging to every era of Chinese history.

The man waited.

Another huff, to indicate his patience wore thin.

"Why, yes. I am traveling alone." She pushed her shoulders back a tad, then added, "One ticket, please."

The train man shook his head. His hand swept across the counter in front of him, pushing aside a small book and a pen with a black barrel. Jots of ink covered the countertop, and matched the dark spots on his fingertips.

"Nope."

Lin blinked.

Her ancestors hadn't overcome pillagers, won battles, and led her people for thousands of years just so she could be turned away by a grubby, sour-faced little man with blackened fingers.

"One ticket west, please." She placed her opened bag on the ledge of wood on her side of the window. Steel bars separated them, but she stared through the barricade with renewed determination. "How much will that be?"

"No can do, lady." He smirked as he spoke.

Lady.

The snub hurt. Her English lessons had taught her enough that she recognized an unkindness when it came her way.

Violet had shared that even in the western frontier, women were treated with politeness by good-hearted men. They were called ma'am or missus when addressed. Even the women who worked at Miss Addie's social club were never disrespected this way.

His use of "lady" in this manner implied that she didn't deserve the same respect a white woman did. The innocuous word, spoken with a sneer got his feelings across.

A slow heat spread across her. Up her chest and neck, and along her cheeks, the fire of humiliation that did nothing to erase the cold the snowy weather had wrapped her in. If anything, this increase in temperature only chilled her further, right down all the layers of her being and straight to her bones.

If I fall, I'll surely crack. Just like one of the icicles hanging from the eaves outside.

She would not fall. Or crack. Or give in to the shame that this man tried to foist upon her. No, she would not give in to prejudice meted out because of her place of origin.

Her people were royalty. And she, the last Jade Princess.

No smarmy little western peasant would make her feel diminished. She would not have it!

"I don't believe you heard me correctly." She kept her voice even and well-modulated, the way Violet had taught. In her head, though, she screamed into the ticket man's face. "I said I need to purchase a one-way ticket to the furthest point west that this rail line serves. Now, how much is the ticket?"

Lin's insides quivered, but she kept the hand poised over the opening of her reticule as steady as possible. It shook a bit, but just. And since the man's beady eyes were locked on hers, she didn't think he'd notice.

"And I said no."

She narrowed her eyes. "I need to purchase a ticket, sir." The word "sir" got a sneer similar to the way he'd said "lady" when speaking with her. It had an effect, because her opponent furrowed his brow when she spoke. "Now, how much will that ticket cost?"

"Is there a problem wit' your hearin'? Or do you Chi-nee don't unnerstan' English?" He turned and spat. "I ain't sellin' any tickets to no Chi-nee, do ya hear me? Just ain't gonna do it, so you can take your tiny feet an' get outta my railway office."

A wave of despair washed over Lin. Here she was, still in Wylder, and a wall of opposition thwarted her plans. How on earth could she think she would get back home with this much prejudice against her? Bad enough that being a woman in a man's world made life difficult, but being a foreigner in English-speaking society made it doubly hard. And this worm of a man didn't even speak English well enough to pass any of the third-year language examinations held in the Wylder School!

Her fingers clenched. She had to get on the next train. She had already left a note for Violet and broken off her relationship with Wei. If she returned now, surely they would find a way to keep her from her destiny.

Well, she had two options. She could either begin walking and hope the snowstorm didn't kill her before she reached the next westward station or find a way to get on the train. It was scheduled to arrive within the half hour and wouldn't remain in the station longer than necessary to unload any freight and passengers.

She would be on the train when it left Wylder, even if it meant she had to stow away.

The man on the other side of the grate looked immobile, but everyone had a price. Traveling with her brother from China, she had learned that. She hated to dip into the funds she had saved, but if it was the only way to sway the horrid person's stand and get him to sell her passage…

A smile. Her grandmother always said a woman's position often became elevated when she offered a congenial expression, so Lin forced the edges of her lips upward and tried to hide her true feelings.

"Perhaps we have gotten off on the wrong foot." She widened her smile and tipped her chin, hoping the demure attitude would soften his black heart. "I need a ticket on the train. It is due shortly and will depart quickly, and you will never see me again. But please, I need to purchase a ticket."

"Did ya not hear me, Chi-nee?" His voice grew louder with every syllable.

Lin hated herself for it, but she flinched.

"I am not sellin' no ticket on this here Union Pacific Railway to no Chi-nee! Now git yerself outta my train station afore I call fer the sheriff."

Call for the sheriff? Lin had no doubt that Sheriff Branch Wylder would have a fit if he saw how this man treated her. She and the sheriff had always been on good terms. He kept the town running smoothly, without any of the wild western behavior that troubled so many other frontier towns. Well, without too much of it, anyway. She and the Bloom sisters had spoken of his superior duties on more than one occasion.

But she couldn't let Sheriff Wylder see her now. Not when she was trying so desperately to leave town without anyone finding out.

Well, if she had to pay extra for a ticket, she would. Her fingers dived into the reticule and closed around her money purse. Before she could pull it from the recesses, a voice came from behind her.

"You will sell this woman a ticket." The voice, so low and strong, sent a shiver up her spine. "What is the cost for a one-way ride to the furthest station on this line?"

The man behind the counter looked beyond her, so she turned. The man in the black duster stood a foot away. His hat still shadowed his face, but his stance was formidable. The man stood six feet at least, a solid wall of black that looked impenetrable.

Maybe it was the steel window or perhaps the ticket man was just plain dumb, but he turned and spat again. Then, he gave a sneer that exposed a row of blackened teeth. Had the man tried to be more disagreeable looking, it would have been difficult. And if he attempted to have a more unlikeable nature, that, too, would be hard to accomplish. Both of those appeared to come easily and naturally to him.

"I ain't sellin' no tickets to no Chi-nee. Now iff'n she were a man who'd stand in the back car and not raise no fuss, mebbe I would. But a female travelin' alone on the railway? Nope. It ain't good fer folks to see that kind of riffraff ridin' our cars."

The man behind her widened his stance and pushed the edges of his duster open. Across his broad chest lay a pair of ammunition belts, filled with cartridges. Black leather holsters hung at his hips with the handles to matching pistols pointed out so they were ready to draw.

In the distance, a train whistle sounded.

"That little speech just cost you the price of a fare." A shift brought the man in black's fingertips within touching distance of the polished gun handles. "Now you're goin' to write this woman a ticket to ride that train. It's coming into this station mighty quick, and I expect those dirty fingers of yours to make out one of those tickets just as fast." He spread his own fingers wide, and at least one of his knuckles cracked.

"But—" The ticket man's face showed as round and pale as an October moon.

"No buts, pal. You've got no one to blame for this turn of events but yourself." A second round of stretching and cracking of the big hands cut the air. The rumble of the approaching train sounded louder and the floorboards shook. "Now, the ticket."

With a shaking hand, the employee filled out the ticket form and tore it from the pad. He pushed it across the wooden countertop.

Lin took it without a word. What could she say? The Union Pacific man clearly despised her and she imagined the price of her fare would come from his wages. And the stranger behind her? Men only helped women like her when they expected something in return. While she had never been in the position before, she knew the way of the world. She had been willing to pay extra for her ticket, but with coin, not her body.

Now she had to figure out how to evade the man in black's expectation for payment.

On a train. The one that had just screeched to a stop outside.

With a small tip of her chin, Lin pulled her gaze upward. The man who had secured her passage still had his hat brim pulled low and didn't acknowledge her silent gratitude. He turned and walked toward the door leading to the platform. Not wanting to give the nasty man behind the counter another chance to disparage her, she followed the other out into the cold.

Better to take her chances with someone who helped her get out of Wylder than the one intent on holding her back.

Chapter 4

The empty passenger windows as the locomotive stopped showed that the train was not full, which came as a pleasant surprise. Lin had only ever ridden during the warm months, when space came at a premium due to the large number of passengers either moving westward or visiting others who had settled the frontier. Then, the train could be noisy and smelly, filled with not only humans but any assortment of animal passengers, as well.

She had ridden in the nice cars near the front of the train with the Bloom sisters when they had gone on short excursions. An enjoyable way to travel and comfortable, too. But now, on her own and with the sting of the man's disgust over her heritage lying heavy on her, Lin decided not to attempt to sit in the nice section.

It took only a few minutes for freight to be unloaded from the cars that carried it. No passengers alighted. The station master, who still gave her and the stranger a wide berth but a nasty glare, signed some paperwork on a clipboard with a uniformed Union Pacific employee who disembarked from the train. When it became clear that the train would depart shortly, they moved to board.

Lin hesitated, then looked up at her companion. The angle of his Stetson concealed most of his features, and his duster fell closed against the weather, but she noticed his angular chin. A stubble on his cheeks showed he hadn't shaved in days.

"Thank you for helping me."

She thought he wasn't going to reply, but after a long pause he nodded. "You're welcome, ma'am."

It took every bit of courage left in her, but she had to ask. "What, ah, what do I owe you for that help?"

The train blew its whistle, designed to move them from the platform onto the vehicle, but the man lingered. Finally, he pushed the hat brim back and met her gaze with eyes that were so dark she thought she might see the night sky in them.

He shook his head. "You don't owe me anything."

The train whistle cut the air again. "Well, you are a very kind man. Thank you."

"Never mistake a kindness for a sign that someone is kind. I am not a good man, ma'am. Not anymore." As the last fell from his lips, he adjusted his hat and held a hand toward the steps leading to the railway car. "We'd best board now. We don't want to be left in Wylder for another week, do we?"

Lin scrambled onto the train, making the ledge between cars just as the wheels began to roll. The man leapt on, for an instant hanging between the train and the depot in the snowy air.

She turned for the back of the train.

No, she did not want to remain in Wylder for another week. Not another minute, even. It was too painful.

Her heart broke as the wheels rumbled on the track, but there was no other way for her. Leaving the place that felt like home and heading back to the land where duty waited sucked the joy from her soul, but she would not falter. She could not.

When she stepped between the cars to look for a seat

in one of the less desirable ones, the man pushed open the door to the car they had boarded. She glanced over her shoulder as he disappeared into the coach, wondering what made a man describe himself the way he had. She couldn't fathom what he had done to give him such a low opinion of himself. If he was truly a bad man, why had he helped her?

There were so many mysteries hidden in humanity, she couldn't hope to discern every one of them. Why, she couldn't even figure out the workings of her own heart and mind, so trying to uncover why others did what they did was surely a waste of her time.

And that time? If the dream she had been having for the past month was any indication of the state of affairs in her homeland, time was short. She had to get back and save the people she had left behind. They needed her, she was sure of it.

The first car she entered wasn't full at all, but there were two clusters who had children with them. And one group's youngsters were three little boys who were mid-jump from seat to seat when she walked through.

Their exuberant cries and laughter would get on anyone's nerves if endured for hours. And the scent of a dirty diaper added to her decision to keep looking for a more inviting train car.

She pulled the door at the end of the section open. The train moved at a good clip now, and wind and snow rushed by just beyond the platform between the cars so she did not rush. Climbing from one car to the other gave her heart a jolt, but she did it, and with a grateful sigh, slid the next one's door open and stepped inside.

This section, like the last, had plenty of room available for passengers, but as she made her way toward the far end, a woman glanced up and squinted her eyes when she saw Lin. The other, whose gray tendrils escaped her dark hat, looked at her as if she were a bit of pus on a festering wound, so deplorably nasty she assaulted the senses. As she approached, the train lurched and Lin's hip hit the back of the seat on the other side of the woman who now did nothing to disguise her aversion.

For an instant, Lin toyed with the idea of sitting down directly across the aisle from the disapproving passenger. It would serve her right, and force her to either check herself or move.

But she'd had enough drama for one day, so she righted herself and pressed on. Perhaps the next car would be more welcoming.

It wasn't. And the following one wasn't, either.

Lin finally took a seat in a car far back in the train, a few before the freight boxes. She had walked between so many moving cars that the burst of trepidation to step from one to another had vanished.

She sank into a seat beside the window and looked out. The sky had turned dark, and snow fell in fat flakes. The storm didn't look as if it would pass quickly, but she didn't care. She had nowhere and everywhere to go, all at once. But this part of her journey wasn't in her control. Hopefully the train would not get into a wreck, like the horrible crash that had happened a while back just outside Wylder. If it didn't, she would be closer to finding her way home. And if it did, well, she would have to figure out how to move forward.

But for now, she rested against the seat and breathed. Sadness tinged with relief, as thick as the snow beyond the glass pane beside her, filled her with emotions that she could not begin to identify. Not in her mother tongue, and certainly not in English.

Nothing prepared a soul for this kind of heartbreak. Nothing.

****

Firelight danced off the tapestries hanging against the fortress' thick stone walls. They kept drafts to a minimum during the cold winter months and offered a layer of coolness to the dampness brought by wet summers. Now, they served their purpose while reminding the occupants of the space of their long illustrious history and distinguished ancestors.

Lin's gaze fixed on the scene that she loved the most. A woman sat atop a section of the Great Wall, looking regal in dark blue robes and crimson slippers. On her head, a spray of red roses tucked into the silver braid that circled over her wise gaze. The undulations of the fire's glow gave the appearance that the woman and wall floated on a sea of golden liquid.

She had no doubt that any of her female ancestors could hover above land that way if they wanted to. All her life, she had been told the stories of greatness achieved by those who went before…and schooled in the expectations the current royalty had for her own life.

But she knew the truth. No matter how hard she tried to be like those whose bloodline she carried forth, she would never be equal to the tasks she'd been born to own. She could comply, agree, learn, practice, do, and be all the things that were part of her duties, but she would never be good enough.

She would never hover above the Great Wall on the currents brought by fire dance. Never.

Still, she stared. Willing herself to believe in herself,

the way her grandmother urged her to. To believe she could fly, the way the other women in her family had done.

"Little Jade Princess, you know what it is you must do. Yet you press your feet in the rocks, trying to grow roots where there isn't soil to support you."

She shook her head. No, that wasn't right. She had roots—roots that went back thousands of years, deep into the sacred earth of their beloved land.

"It will not change the truth, to deny the facts that way." Her grandmother's voice took a hard edge to it, one that rarely showed itself. But there was no mistaking the steel behind the words now. "You cannot find true happiness in a lie. There is no truth in avoiding what cannot be changed. And one's stubborn refusal to see the way forward can only lead to sadness."

Sadness? The move being foisted upon her now would lead to heartbreak. She could almost guarantee the fact. It might be for someone else, this banishment to a distant land, but not for her.

Never for her.

"I will die of a shattered heart if I have to leave." She hitched a breath and swallowed her pride. "I will die, do you hear me? Without you, and my homeland and people, I will not be able to draw a breath. Never again, not one single breath."

The shadows deepened and her grandmother's eyes slipped into the darkness, but she did not need to see them to know their gaze had not changed. Her words, the ones spoken from the depths of her soul, made no impact on the older woman.

"You are young, my Little Jade Princess. The only way for you to live, is to leave. And the only way for you

to love and breathe, is to go. You will be carried on the breath of your ancestors to the moment of your destiny."

"The moment of my destiny? But I don't even understand what that means!"

The matriarch turned to leave. Lin reached out a hand to stop her, but instead of catching the shoulder of the embroidered silk jacket, her fingers clutched air.

One step put distance between them. A second, even more.

When her grandmother began to take the third step, Lin screamed.

"No!" The single word tore at her throat.

Her grandmother paused, tipping her face toward the tapestry that still looked as if their ancestor danced above the Great Wall with fire licking her toes.

"Do not return to China. Once you are gone, stay gone."

Another pause, but the woman stood still so Lin waited.

Finally, a sigh. "You do not believe me now, my girl, but you will see. Your destiny is not here. Your heart may always belong to this land and our people, but it will not begin to beat until you meet its other half. And that half, it is far from here." She took a step, increasing the distance between them. "So, go. And stay gone."

"No, please..."

Tears slid down her cheeks as she watched her grandmother walk out of the room.

Her parting words echoed in Lin's head.

Stay gone.

Stay gone.

Stay gone.

They came over and over, an admonition that

sounded louder with each passing moment.
The words had a harder edge to them.
They shook her to the very center of her body.
Stay.
Gone.
Stay.
Go—

A jolt shook her awake. Her eyes flew open. The first thing she saw, a wall of well-worn dirty black fabric that fluttered near her face as she blinked.

Then, a hand pushed the fabric, which turned out to be a jacket flap, back. Now, inches from her nose, another patch of dirty fabric. The aroma of it made her nose crinkle in disgust.

A man's crotch. Right in front of her, and the man who owned it didn't show any sign of moving. She wrinkled her nose when an unpleasant smell invaded her head. Surely the man whose private parts were inches from her face hadn't bathed in a while.

Another jolt, the train thudding over some faulty bit of track, perhaps, made her sway. Her right shoulder bounced off a woman's form.

When she'd closed her eyes, there had been no one on the bench next to her. She glanced at the other woman, gave an apologetic nod, then faced the man again. She tipped her head back, and saw a stranger as grimy as his clothing.

"Well, lookee here." His cheek puffed out, a wad of tobacco the size of a plum tucked beside his teeth. He surveyed Lin before dropping his attention on her seatmate. "My two foreign ladies, just lookin' fer a friend."

Oh, good heavens, didn't any man in this territory

have sense enough to steer clear of unfamiliar women? Did they all think women waited for them to come along to grace them with their presence?

And "my"? Whatever could he mean by that?

Her mind swept back to a moment beside the river back in Wylder. She and one of the Bloom sisters had been picking berries, when an unsavory man came upon them and tried—no, she wouldn't think of it. He hadn't had his way with either of them and had ended up dead for his trouble.

The man smirking at her reminded her of the man they'd killed. The same nefarious gleam in his dark eyes. And, the stench of him. An assault to the senses that turned her stomach and sent bile rising to burn the back of her throat. The only difference? This man had come from China. She recognized one of her own people, even one who had no respect for those who shared a homeland.

"Please leave us alone." She spoke quietly, so he wouldn't feel as if he had to prove himself, but loudly enough for him to hear above the sound of the rails and talk in the car. It had filled since she'd boarded, and bits of conversation in several languages reached her ears. When the man didn't move, she added, "We want no trouble, so please leave us."

"Oh, I'll leave ya, all right. I'll leave ya both when I'm done with ya, and not afore."

The woman beside her stiffened. Lin placed a hand on the other's nearest elbow, hoping to show strength in numbers. To her surprise, her companion tilted her head back and gave the man a smile.

"It is good that you found us."

The man blinked. Then, he burped, sending a wave

of stale alcohol-infused air washing over them.

Beside her, the woman went on as if the man brought a breeze scented by wildflowers instead of the reeking, gut-turning reality of the situation. Lin had all she could do to keep from putting a hand over her nose. How the other summoned a smile was beyond her.

"Oh, you do not remember me? We met earlier, I am sure of it." A soft, almost flirtatious, laugh accompanied the words.

Again, the man blinked, clearly confused by the turn of events. "Oh, I remember ya, all right. I jes' didn't think ya'd be so happy ter see me, is all."

The woman beside her gave another small laugh. It sounded a tad wobbly. "Oh, of course I am happy to see you. Why, you know I am."

"'Bout time yer came 'round." Another belch and a fresh wave of stomach-turning fumes.

Not to be put off by the man's rude behavior, the woman nudged Lin over to create a space beside her on the seat. When she patted the spot, enticing the man to sit, Lin nearly stood up to leave. But how could she go, leaving another woman to deal with this stinky, horrid man? She couldn't, so she stayed put, but wished the man hadn't sat so close. Even with the other's body between them, the stench from his person turned her stomach.

She tried to pretend she didn't sit in a crowded railway car, in a maelstrom of odors that made any Chinese barnyard smell like paradise. Her concentration shifted to the man she left behind in Wylder, bringing a lump to her throat and chasing away every other thought—including those borne on the smell of unwashed bodies.

Wei. How could she have left him? When she had

fled China with her brother, she had believed it would be the hardest thing she would ever have to do. It had been so painful, to turn from all she knew and loved and head toward the unknown.

Now she realized that while it had been difficult, it didn't come close to bringing pain like she felt from leaving Wei behind. Her very soul ached, deep within her where she thought only bones and organs resided. Deeper even than her heart, the place she'd believed to be the very center of herself.

She touched a fingertip to the spot on her blouse between her collarbones, where the jade burial tile nestled against her skin. She wondered if a similar agony came before her death to the princess who wore the rest of the ancient burial costume. *Perhaps this is how a body feels just before leaving this world to go to the next.* Surely such a deep, intense hurt must cause one to stop breathing.

Breathing. It still came with a price. The man sat too close for Lin to remain for much longer. They were nearing a depot if murmurings from those nearby were correct. She would change seats when the train stopped. The stench from the man, who had finally gone silent now that he sat beside the other woman, would not become more bearable with the passing miles. If anything, he smelled worse now. An odd metallic odor wafted from him, one that hadn't been there when he stood looking down at them.

The train slowed. Fellow passengers stood, reached for their bags. Footsteps shook the wooden floorboards and the aisle filled. She waited a few minutes, as the first wave of people exited onto the platform, before she turned to the woman beside her.

She planned to tell her she couldn't stay in the seat and ask her to come to another car with her, but the expression on the other's face froze the thoughts in Lin's mind. Something was wrong. Terribly wrong.

The woman hauled her up when she stood. Lin opened her mouth, but had no chance to speak.

"We must go." The other pushed her none too gently toward the aisle as she grabbed both of their bags. "Now."

Lin relieved the other of her bag and shot her a scowl. As she did, she knew it impolite, but what on earth made her companion think it okay to shove her out of her seat this way?

"What are you doing?" She planted her feet. "Why are you pushing me?" Her left hip met the edge of the seat, sending pain from the point of contact. Surely a bruise would form, she'd hit that hard.

"Go, go, go!" Another shove from the woman whose petiteness hid her strength. "We must go!"

Confusion, as well as the desire to not bounce off another part of the train car, made Lin step into the aisle. The crowd had thinned, so she glanced back. First at the woman practically stepping on her skirt tail. Then, to the smelly man.

He sat slumped in the seat, his hat low over his face. Her gaze fell to the dark spot on his side. To the wet dollops on the seat.

Then, to her female acquaintance. The woman met and held her gaze as the truth washed over Lin.

The man was dead. The woman who pushed her to the exit had killed him.

And somehow, without even knowing how it happened, Lin had become an accomplice to a murder.

She moved quickly toward the train platform, suddenly not caring where they were—or what she would do when she got there.

Just as well, she thought. What could she say to a woman who had just cold-bloodedly killed a man? She looked over her shoulder for any sign of railroad employees or U.S. Marshals behind them. She half expected they would show up and take them both to whatever passed for a jail in this noisy town.

Where were they? She looked for a sign or even a newspaper headline, but there weren't any indications of where they had gotten themselves to.

Trouble, she thought. They were in trouble, and up to their necks!

****

The gemstone shop Wei owned was not a large space. Like most buildings on Wylder Street, the modest wood-frame structure met its owner's needs, without any ostentatious trimmings some of the bigger businesses offered. It sat tiny by comparison to the mercantile, but it provided adequate room for him to conduct his business. Now, the space closed in on him, and the air, usually sweetly scented by the array of tinctures and herbs lining the shelves on one whitewashed wall, burned his lungs.

The anger rushing through his body came as a shock. Sweat slicked his brow and heat crept up his neck. In his temples, twin pulses beat so hard, surely they must make the skin above the arteries move.

Back in China, he had loved being a physician and knowing about how the human body worked. His schooling taught him that unchecked emotions, such as the ones gripping him now, were unhealthy. They almost never led to positive consequences, and often were harmful to their owner. He had to get a grip on his temper before he hurt himself.

But deep down, where he spoke only absolute truth to himself, the loathing for his actions and the harm he had inflicted made him want to feel a retaliatory punch. He deserved what he was given, and he welcomed retribution.

Rarely, if ever, had Wei been so furious. Sure, the injustices the world dealt a man of his ethnicity walking through a sea of otherwise-tinted faces often came with a price, but he didn't allow any of that to alter his behavior. Or his opinion of his fellow man.

His own stupidity, his mule-headed stubbornness, and his inability to see the severity of a situation brought so much fury he could barely think.

But he must think, now more than ever. The life of a woman he adored and the future they should be planning had been put in jeopardy. By his own hand, he had risked it all. Everything that mattered to him could already be gone.

He forced himself to stand still, to take a deep breath and calm the frantic beating in his chest. Slow and steady, he thought. Just breathe.

"Wei? Please, please answer me!" A hand on his forearm squeezed, so he turned his head to see who implored him. In his frenzy, he had forgotten where he stood. Now, Violet Bloom's striking amethyst-colored eyes were so wide and round they would be laughable if the circumstances were different. Instead, they were filled with fear. Remorse shot through him as he realized she had been talking with him, and he hadn't heard a word she had said.

Not one word. His rage at his own stupidity had consumed him so, his body remained in place while his head wandered miles away.

"I am sorry." He ran his free hand over his head, down the long braid that hung over his shoulder. The familiar gesture pushed some stress back, but just a touch. "I did not hear you. My mind, it was…elsewhere."

The woman released her hold on him, letting her hand drop to her side for only a moment before she caught the two together and wrung them near her waist. Her concern for Lin couldn't have been more evident. She had gone pale, almost as white as winter snow.

"I understand. But we need to keep our wits about us, mustn't we? I mean, if we are to find precious Lin, we need to stay the course."

The course? He didn't point out that there was no course, that he'd yet to pull together a plan, and that even when he did, her wits weren't going to be useful, whether she kept them controlled, or not.

But Violet—all the Bloom sisters, actually—loved Lin. Not in the sense he did, but they loved her like one of their own. Like a sister, and that bond could be stronger than any other.

He must concede to her concerns and somehow soothe her frayed nerves. And do it fast, so he could leave Wylder.

"Yes, of course. You are right, we must be calm." He paused, then asked, "Are you sure Lin did not tell you anything about the exact passage she and her brother took to get from China to here?"

A fast head shake sent a lock of hair from her updo. And that, the flying hairpin, showed just how completely the woman feared she would never see Lin again. The sisters had a reputation for being the women with the tightest-placed hairpins in town. None ever had a lock out of place, under ordinary circumstances. Men joked about it (discreetly, of course) and women envied the talent.

But never, in all the time Violet Bloom had been in Wylder, had her hair come undone in public.

No time to contemplate women's hairstyles. He had to leave town. Every moment let the distance increase and lessened the odds of his finding the only woman who mattered to him.

"Nothing. She never spoke about going back." She brushed the hair off her cheek, then tangled her fingers together again. "Lin told me she's a Black Pearl, the one rarity that comes from being the sole remaining member of a family. She said that going back to the place they fled would be sure death." Her voice caught on the last words.

He sucked in a breath. Thankfully, the herbal tea he'd consumed first thing after waking had cleared the dull ache overindulgence in liquor brought. A twist in his gut, when he thought about what he'd nearly done last night, brought a shiver.

Violet reached a hand out but paused before she touched him. "Are you ill?" She knit her brows, and her cheeks reddened. "I, um, well I heard you had a, well, a hard night. Have you, um…well, do you think…"

It hit him that she searched for a delicate way to ask if he had picked up a disease from the whore he had visited last night. It shamed him that she knew. It shamed his ancestors that he had been inside that sort of establishment, even if it was one as pristine and high-class as Wylder's Social Club.

He would be forever grateful that he had not indulged his base desires with a strange woman. He had never paid for intimacy and would rather be celibate for the remainder of his life than begin to do that now.

Not trusting himself to not stumble over an explanation, he gave a sharp head shake. Then, unable to meet the schoolteacher's gaze, he said, "I did nothing that would give me any sort of illness last night—other than the hangover I deserved when I woke this morning. I assure you, Miss Bloom, I slept last night. Nothing more." He raised his face and met her embarrassed stare. "I swear, I was not unfaithful to Miss Sun Lin. Even though we are not married, I am faithful to her in my heart and ways. That will never change."

Violet nodded, a sound like relief escaping her. She did not comment, but moved to a more pressing topic.

"Thomas and Theo, my brother-in-law, will go with you to find Lin. And the sheriff can't leave Wylder, but he said he has a few men who can be spared to help you search."

When Violet showed up in his shop, he had been packing his saddlebag. It lay open on the table where he usually created elaborate gemstone jewelry. Where had he left off? Oh, right. He reached for the bundle of dried herbs and fruit he'd taken from the cupboard. They would come in handy if Lin was unwell when he located her.

And he would find her. If he did it with his final breath, he would gaze upon the beautiful woman again.

Or die trying to make it happen.

The bundle tucked into the bag, he considered the helpfulness of having others ride with him. While he hated that he would take them from their homes and families, they were a community, and that's what being part of one meant. They offered assistance when necessary. The truth, that he could search on his own and maybe take much longer to find Lin, decided him. More manpower meant a broader search, and he would humble himself to get to her.

"I am grateful. But I will be leaving momentarily." When Violet blinked in surprise, he added, "I cannot wait. Every minute counts, you see."

A tight smile turned the corners of her lips upward. "I do see." A tilt of her head at the sound of hoofbeats outside the shop's front door. They came so fast and hard, the snow did not hide their arrival. "And I believe your riding companions see, too."

****

Two nights in a room above a saloon had eaten a considerable amount of Lin's funds. She had planned carefully, and saved for months for the trip, but had never thought she would be stranded in a dusty town with a woman who she had seen murder a man. Not even in her wildest nightmare could she see this happening.

Although now that she knew what motivated her new friend, she didn't blame her, not one bit, for doing what she'd done. In fact, her quick thinking and brave actions probably saved Lin from brutality at the man's hands.

She sighed, thinking of how she learned that bad people were no different in this new land than they were in her homeland. When she and Mei finally left the crush at the train station behind, she had ducked into a narrow dirty alley and pulled the other woman into the gloom with her.

"You killed that man," she hissed. Her gaze pinned

the woman's. She saw no remorse in the dark brown eyes staring back at her and for an instant wondered if this might be a big mistake. She stood inches from a killer, in a dark confined, secluded space. Maybe she would die next!

But the woman didn't deny her actions, and her tone touched Lin's heart.

"I did. I had to…" A tremble in the words. "He was a bad man, a very bad man." Another wobble to the explanation, before she sucked in a deep breath and held it for a moment. When she spoke again, her voice came out with some steel behind it. "He hurt me, a long time he held me captive, and he hurt me. I would not allow him to do it anymore, so I ran. And I knew that if he took me, he would try to take you, too." She paused, then pulled up the edge of her blouse to expose her side.

Just above her slender waist, a jagged wound. The edges of the skin were closing together, but it looked red hot and painful. It took a second for Lin to realize what caused the damage.

She raised her gaze. "He did this to you?"

The woman tried to pull her arm away, but Lin did not release her grip.

Finally, a nod.

"That man cut you like this?" She looked back down, then met the other's gaze. She saw pain there, but also triumph. And, the strength of the woman. "Did he use a knife? Or was it something else?" She suspected the latter, from the jaggedness of the cut.

"A bottle. He got angry when I refused to do… When he was drunk he made me do…things."

"He assaulted you?"

As she carefully lowered her blouse and tucked it

back into the waistband of her skirt, she nodded. "Yes. Many times." She smoothed a hand down the front of her skirt and dropped her gaze to the ground. They stood beside discarded papers, and the alley smelled like it got regular use as a latrine, but she doubted the woman noticed. Her mind had gone off to a place that, from the pinched line between her eyebrows and thin set of her lips, brought pain with the memories.

"Was he your husband?"

"No. I would never marry a filthy pig like that. No. It is a long story, and I will tell you all of it, but for now can we just go? Find someplace safe?" She glanced out of the alley, at the crowd, then back to Lin. "He said he would save me, keep me safe, when my husband died. We came from Tianjin after the riot in eighteen hundred seventy. We were both—" She raised her chin and brought a defiant tone to her voice. "—Christian. My husband said it was not safe for us at home, so we came here. And we were happy..." She clenched her eyes closed tightly, as if she could see the truth of what she lost seared on her retinas. A sigh, and she opened her eyes. "We were happy, until he got sick. When he died, I was lost. I did not know what to do. And that man, he came to the church where we were members. He made promises, offered safety, but he lied."

Lin's blood ran cold. How could anyone be so cruel as to prey on a widow? A woman alone in a strange land, who lost the one person she had been willing to cross the globe with?

Again, it hit her that cruelty existed everywhere. It wasn't only Chinese hit men, anxious to steal a family's legacy and lead its people, that brought evil to the world.

"I am sorry." She laid a hand on the other's arm. "I

was a child when the Tianjin Massacre took place, but I heard about it from my elders. It is a crime, an evilness in the world, that makes people think their way of living, of worshiping, or thinking is the only way. I have never understood how people could kill while calling themselves faithful to anything." She scrambled to recall how many died during the anti-Christian event. More than a dozen, she knew. She met the woman's gaze. "You must have been very young yourself."

That brought a smile, for which Lin was grateful. It chased away some of the pain their conversation caused and smoothed over the furrows near her companion's brow. "Oh, yes. We were married very young. You see, we were playmates as children, so we always knew we would marry. My parents gave permission, so we did not wait. I will be forever grateful that we had that time, that we did not put off our life together until we were older. It was a blessing, those years we had."

A blessing of a life turned into a nightmare, Lin thought. She did not need to hear any more to believe that what happened on the train had been justified. Any woman who endured abuse like what showed on this one's body should not be condemned for doing whatever she needed to do to get free from her abuser. And she felt certain that she had been saved, as well. She had no doubt that the man would try to take her with him whenever he deemed it safe to do so. After all, two protesting Chinese women resisting a man of their own kind would only be seen as a public nuisance, not something others should involve themselves in. No help would have come for them, had the dead man insisted they get off the train with him.

No, she didn't need to hear another word to know

that the woman standing with her was not a murderer as much as she was a blessing herself. She'd saved Lin from harm, and that brought a surge of gratitude.

She made a fast decision. They couldn't stay in the alley forever, and it wouldn't be wise to stay in this town. If the man's body hadn't already been discovered, and she thought it must have been by now, it would be found soon. And that would bring questions, and anyone who had seen him while they were on the train would be able to tell train officials that he had been with two women. Two Chinese women.

They had to put some distance between themselves and the dead man. But how? Her new friend had a serious wound which most likely weakened her. She couldn't travel by foot. And they couldn't get back on the train. Even if it hadn't left the station, the evidence of their crime wouldn't move on its own.

The rumble of wooden wheels in the lane beyond the alley gave her an idea. They might not be able to catch a stagecoach, not if there weren't any passing through in the very near future, but that didn't mean they couldn't find a wagon driver willing to give them a ride.

"Come on." Lin tucked her arm through the other's and took a step toward the lane. "We need to get moving." She stopped as she realized she didn't know the other's name. "We haven't been introduced. I'm Lin, and you are?"

Finally, a smile that looked genuine. "Mei. My name is Mei."

Fitting, Lin thought.

"Beautiful," she murmured, translating the word from their native tongue.

Mei's smile grew. "Yes, at least to my parents."

Chapter 5

Wei put his shoulder down against the wind and urged the horse forward. The snowy conditions in Wylder were behind them, having given way to the skin-shearing wind of the western plains. He almost preferred the cold to the brutality of the relentless sting of grit tearing into every bit of exposed skin.

Had he been alone, fatigue would have sent him toppling from his saddle, but since the others were with him, he'd been forced to stop and rest. Sleep was an elusive bedfellow, and even the glow of a campfire couldn't chase the fear from his soul. And now, as the hours wore on, doubt played tricks with his mind. Doubt over his ability to find the love of his life. And a mountain of it when he thought of whether he would be able to convince her to stay with him in this land.

If she refused to remain, he would go with her, back to China. He didn't want to do it, but he would if that was what it took to keep her.

They had been riding four days already, stopping in every town along the rail line looking for some sign of Lin. So far, nothing. Not even a glint of hope, a whisper from one person who may have seen her.

She had vanished. Or rather she had melted into the stream of nameless faces that moved across the western frontier. Women weren't expected to be chaperoned out here the way he understood was common in other places.

So many females running from bad situations, others widowed through hardships met along the trail or as part of their homesteading experiences, and more striking out, the way men did, in search of a better life. So a sea of females on the move, and hardly anyone taking notice of them.

Which, of course, proved frustrating for Wei. He knew he saw one woman as above all others and through the eyes of a man in love, but it seemed completely unreasonable that no one—not one single, solitary person—had noticed the beautiful Sun Lin. A princess passed among them, and these peasants weren't smart enough to see the shine in the midst of all this red dust.

Beside him, Thomas Harvey leaned from his saddle and raised his voice to be heard above the whistling wind. "Wei, we've got to stop soon. I know you want to find her—we all do—but the horses need to get some rest."

The truth couldn't be denied. They had been pushing both man and beast for days now.

He glanced up at their surroundings, and snow hit his eyes. A wall of white, not so thick it obliterated the distant mountaintops, but it meant business. The ridges on the landscape were softened by snow, turning tumbleweeds that usually sped across the plains pushed by the prairie breezes into mounds pressed against boulders. The view could have been worse, but it also could have been much better. The weather did not encourage travel.

For an instant, he considered trading his mount for one at the livery in the next town they hit and continuing on, but idea was more stubborn determination than logic. To leave the others behind and keep going would be an insult, and the men who'd sacrificed their own comfort to help him deserved more than that. And he felt certain that he'd drop from exhaustion himself if he didn't get some sleep.

"Agreed." He kept his gaze on the terrain ahead and nodded to the horizon. "Looks like a town up ahead. When we get to it, let's unsaddle the horses and find some food."

They all would fare better with full bellies.

"And some rest, my friend. We won't need much, but you've got to admit we'll all be better prepared to search for Lin if we weren't holdin' our eyelids up with toothpicks."

He turned to the man beside him and offered a small smile. "You are a wise man, Thomas. Thank you."

The other shook his head and tipped his hat brim down a touch lower on his forehead. "Aw, I'm not so wise. Believe me, I've done a lot of stupid things in my time. But we're all set on finding Lin, and it doesn't take much to know that we'll be more up to the task with some hot food in our stomachs and few hours of shut-eye." He shot a gaze between them. "I hate to say it, but you've got more wrinkles on your face than the desert has cactus. No sleep and too much worry will kill a man, and I'm not wanting to be in the position of explaining to your lady friend how we let you get in such a sorry state. Because we will find her, Wei. We're not giving up, just resting up."

The town drew closer with every step, so he shook his head and swallowed hard. He had been hesitant to accept help when he started out to find Lin but was grateful for the men who rode beside him. With no idea how he would ever thank them for what they were doing, he kept his gaze on the horizon as Thomas fell back to speak with the others.

Not giving up, he thought. Not now. Not ever.

****

The sounds in the room had become familiar quickly. Rasp of bristles on wood. The squeak of twine being wrapped around a handle. The soft gasp at a sliced fingertip.

She supposed every woman in the room knew these new noises by now. Some had been here longer than others, but at one point it had been unfamiliar to each of them. They must also recognize the collective futility and hopelessness that permeated the space. Impossible to either hide or deny.

An ache, one that came almost constantly these days, pulled Lin's hand to her chest. She rested it there above her heart. Every beat felt like a protest against going on, a hard thump deep within her that screamed that her current situation wasn't right. That she had gotten in way over her head with no good way forward, no easy way back.

She'd thought her decision would bring peace. Instead, turmoil. It writhed within her, a constant motion that reminded her of the seasickness she had endured on the journey from China. Then, too, an unsettled feeling that began in the tips of her toes, traveled its way into the tummy, and threatened to spill from her. No way to control the sensations, hardly anything to do to stop it once it began.

She hated losing control. On the ship, she had been one of many who were at the mercy of their emotions and physical maladies. But now, without the sea to rock her senseless, she allowed that the turmoil came from within. She generated her own misery, and that almost made her more miserable. Being captive to an outside force wasn't good, but creating the force to make oneself ill wasn't just troubling, but foolhardy.

But foolishness diminishes when a mind rules more solidly than any part of a body. In her case, her mind rode at the back of the mule team, while the steady thump in her chest led the way.

Maybe her heart knew best. Maybe she was drowning in the circumstances of her life, with no hope to swim to safety, let alone happiness. Not for herself, or for those waiting back in the province where she had been born.

The ache increased, and her fingertips massaged the area, rasping over the wash-worn blouse she wore. The work she'd done these past days had turned her hands rough. The skin on her fingertips where she had scraped them working on brooms stung. And the ache in her wrists, from holding the wooden dowel and turning it to attach the bristles, had become a constant companion. She had not known a body could ache this way before now.

Another less-than-ideal circumstance of her current situation brought on by what she had believed the only, and best, option open to her.

And here she sat, surrounded by women in similar situations who probably had similar thoughts that had driven them to make closely matching decisions. So much could go wrong in life, even when one thought they had weighed every possible option and outcome. And life showed its hard side, especially to women who walked its path on their own.

She turned to Mei in time to see the other woman

grimace. A look down to her hands told the painful story. Fingertips injured from hours attaching skin-scraping bristles to wooden sticks, then wrapping heavy twine around them to keep the bristles in place. What had once been soft, supple skin now bore the bloody marks left behind by the tedious work.

"Oh, Mei, your fingers!" Lin dropped a completed broom into the tall wooden pail beside her. Practice had turned her hands nimble; she had more brooms in the pail than she had yesterday, and there were hours left to the afternoon. She rubbed her hands down the front of her skirt, smoothing the tingling skin on the soft muslin. Then, she reached for her friend's work. "Here, let me finish that one for you."

The bristles were in place, so she reached for a length of twine and began wrapping. It wasn't difficult work, and anyone could learn to make a broom in a matter of minutes. But it did mercilessly damage tender skin, especially after endless hours moving the materials between fingertips.

"You cannot do my work for me, Lin." She wiped a bead of blood on a rag and winced. While she could protest, she could not conceal her pain. "You have your own work to do."

The words fell on deaf ears. As a princess, Lin had been born to serve, in one way or another, and it did not escape her memory the lessons she had learned from birth. They might not be in their homeland, but her obligations couldn't be tossed aside regardless of location.

Besides, helping the woman who saved her from whatever murky plan that awful man on the train had in his head wasn't even close to repaying the debt she owed. For the rest of her life, she would be obligated to Mei. Any time she had considered what might have happened had Mei not acted so quickly, terror shot through every cell in her body. The man meant to harm her, and the kind woman beside her had kept her from a horrible fate. How could she ever repay that?

"It is not a hardship for me to help. See? I am nearly finished." She gave one last tug on the twine to be sure it held the working end of the tool securely, then leaned behind the other woman to drop it into Mei's pail. There were not nearly as many completed brooms as there were in Lin's. Once she had finished hers, she would add more to this tally. For now, though, the one she just completed would help. "And I don't mind doing it."

They paused. Around them, tables covered with broom-making supplies and hard wooden stools where dozens of women sat. No carefree, happy chatter could be heard, no laughter or shared confidences. Just the whooshing sound of bristles being aligned around poles. The rasp of twine wrapping it all together. A startled gasp as fingers were pinched or skin torn from hands.

Mei reached for a fresh handful of bristles. "Well, thank you for helping with that one, but you mustn't do my work for me. It isn't fair."

Lin sighed. She wrapped her fingers around a broom handle and squeezed. Fair? Nothing about this nightmare was fair. They'd left that far behind them, and she doubted they would ever live a life that wasn't disadvantageous ever again.

They worked for next to nothing, although the man who paid them at the end of each day acted as if he doled out gold and rainbows rather than miserly compensation. He ran a boardinghouse next to the workplace and some of the women stayed there, so in many instances the cash flowed right back to him. There were whispers among the women that he approached some with offers of extra money for sexual services, but he had not done that with either Lin or Mei. They had agreed that if he did so, they would seek other employment.

She hoped he kept his distance. Work didn't come easily for women like them, and since she had the unexpected rooming expenses when they fled the train, her funds would not take her to China. And she had no intention of leaving Mei behind, so they both needed to work.

As Lin started the next broom, she wondered how they would ever find their way home. Also, where could she call home now? When she had gotten on the train out of Wylder, she had been sure her journey ended back where she had begun, on the soil that her ancestors walked. But now, she wasn't at all sure that she had chosen well. Her heart ached and she would give what was left of the skin on her fingertips to see Wei again. To walk the streets of Wylder, where life didn't make her stomach clench and her pulse race, the way it did here. The further she traveled from Wylder, the less sure she was that she moved in the direction fate meant for her. And, with every day that passed, her yearning to return to the love and safety of Wei's arms grew.

But the truth couldn't be denied. She had left a good man, one who loved her and wanted to make a life with her, without a word. By now he had probably found another woman to share his life, one who wouldn't be so eager to toss him aside for anyone or anything—not even a misguided notion that strangers mattered more than he did.

Because she had realized, in these long, hard hours perched on an unforgiving stool surrounded by women equally, if not more, downtrodden that her determination to return to China had been entirely self-serving. She had convinced herself she returned to serve her people, but that concealed the truth.

Living in Wylder brought joy where there had been so much sorrow. It gave her a new caring community after she had lost everyone. The frontier became more familiar and comfortable than the rolling green hills of her Chinese province. The family she found there made her feel at home.

And all of that scared her. It sent chills all the way to the deepest recesses of her heart so frightening that she had run from all of it.

The last time she had been so happy, she had lost everyone and everything that mattered to her. Finding that joy in Wylder only opened her up to a fresh loss, and rather than take that chance, she had made an excuse and run.

But she wondered if there was any place that she could run to and not be at risk of having happiness snatched away again.

She didn't think so. But that realization came too late. She had already lost Wei and Wylder, and once again sat homeless, unloved, and lost.

Princess or not, she was a woman with no future.

****

Wei slapped his hat against his thigh, turning his head when a small cloud of trail dust rose. He'd breathed in enough grit to clog two sets of lungs. He certainly didn't need any extra, not if he could help it.

At least they had left the snow behind. That was

something to be grateful for.

The long ride on horseback had turned his back tender. His thigh muscles ached. And his wrists screamed their protest every time he moved a hand. He had not been born into a life of physical movement, especially not anything near what he currently undertook. In China, he had lived a life of ease as a child. When he pursued his medical career, he worked, but treating patients did not bring physicality comparable to riding a horse countless miles over often rough terrain.

His body rebelled, but he would not give up. His heart pushed him forward, and even though he had lost a bit of hope that he would find his Jade Princess quickly, he intended to find her. No matter how long it took or how many parts of his body wailed their displeasure, he would find her.

It was the only way. Find Lin and live or die from the grief of losing her.

Branch Wylder, Wylder's sheriff, had sent three men to travel with them. They rode in a loose cluster, each man always on the lookout for a figure in the distance, or worse, a body beside the trail. The men worked one of the ranches just outside town and could be spared during these cold days. January wasn't typically a busy time on any ranch, so workers often took the opportunity to head back home, wherever that happened to be. Others, like the trio traveling with them now, filled the weeks any way they could.

Theo and one of the men rode up beside Wei. He searched his memory for the other man's name. They all looked alike, especially after days on the trail. The heavy jackets they all wore to protect from the unpredictable weather did much to conceal identities as well.

Buck, he thought. Could that be it? Buck...or was it Derrick?

Did it matter? No, it did not. All that counted rested with the fate of one very special woman. Nothing more deserved his energy.

Theo Harvey cleared his throat. "So listen, Wei. Brodrick here says we're comin' up on a smallish town. Just a couple of miles up the trail, a place to stop and grab a hot meal, if nothing else."

Brodrick. That was it.

Theo's Appaloosa stood at least seventeen hands high, a beautiful creature that seemed born to endless treks across the frontier. Now and again, after a long day of riding, one or two of the other horses lagged back, but Theo's never did. As they rode side by side, the animal nickered, as if encouraging Wei's mount to pick up the pace.

Brodrick spoke. "It's nothin' fancy, just a one-horse town with the usual businesses." The words were raspy, as if he'd smoked a thousand cigarettes in his lifetime. Maybe he had, Wei thought. "But there's a few hidey-holes where a woman might take shelter. A boardinghouse, a washing parlor." He hesitated, then added, "A place kinda like Miss Addie's, only not so nice. A little shabbier, if you get my meanin'."

A brothel. Not a clean, respectable (or as respectable as that kind of business can be) operation like the Social Club. He had only been in Miss Addie's establishment that one time, but even with his discernment altered by his dalliance in the Five Star, he recognized that what passed as a brothel in Wylder must be a cut above what went on in other places.

If anyone had suggested that his precious Lin might

take refuge in a house of ill repute a few weeks ago, they would have gotten a black eye for disrespecting her. But as they plodded along, he saw the possibility that Brodrick might be right. If she had nowhere else to shelter, Lin might find herself in such a spot.

When he didn't reply, the other men rushed to clarify.

Theo put a hand out between them, gloved palm up. The leather showed how much the homesteader's hands were used, and how tough homesteading could be. Scrapes and scuffs marred the gloves, but they fit like a second skin on the other's hand. "I'm sure Brodrick is only trying to help, Wei. No one, not any of us, would ever suggest that Miss Lin would…well, you know. That's not what he meant, was it, Broderick?"

"No, not at all!" The man cleared his throat. "I never meant nothing like that. I'm only suggestin' it because a woman on her own might find comfort with other ladies, is all. And we're passin' right by, so what's the harm in pokin' around? I don't mean a bit of disrespect, Wei. I just wanna find your lady and get her back home to Wylder as fast as we can."

"It's what we all want," Theo added. Wei turned and met the man's eyes. Of course, he spoke the truth.

"I'm not offended." He nudged his horse to move faster. "Yes, it's what we need to do, find her and take her home."

He hoped Lin would agree to return to Wylder. If not, he would do whatever it took to stay with her, even abandoning the life he'd made for himself.

Wei met Brodrick's gaze. "How far is this town?"

" 'Bout two miles. Up at the fork, we head south about a mile. There's an old mine down there, went dry almost from the start. But some folks stayed in town." He shrugged, muscular shoulders pulling the dark jacket he wore tight. "Might be someplace someone tryin' to hide might consider. Unless ya know about the mine, ya wouldn't know about the town—or what's left of it."

Two miles. If he was lucky, that's all that separated him from Lin. His arms ached again, but not from the exertion of riding. No, they throbbed with a yearning so powerful he could hardly stand it. He'd give anything to have her in his embrace again. And he didn't care if she had taken to working in a brothel—he would respect anything at all that she had to do to survive. He would not like it if that was the case, but he would accept it and hope to take her from those circumstances. And, he'd make certain she never had to do anything out of desperation ever again.

Two miles. He urged the horse to move faster a second time. Endless days of riding and searching were taking their toll. He had to find Lin, and soon. His heart needed to feel whole again, and it wouldn't until he pulled her close and they figured things out between them.

****

The long room held more than a dozen cots, squeezed into the space with barely room to walk between them. Women working at the broom factory who didn't have homes and refused to stay in the boardinghouse were housed in the building above the workshop. The accommodations were harsh, but they at least had a roof above their heads. A cast-iron belly stove in the corner of the room did little to cut the cold air. The good part of being so tightly jammed into the space, that they generated some heat practically huddled together.

Lin had experienced similar circumstances on the long sea voyage from her homeland. She and her brother had been squashed into the bowels of the big ship they boarded, human cargo that saw little sunlight or fresh air. The biggest difference was the broom ladies weren't subject to the pitching motion of the ocean. There wasn't a pervading stench of vomit, either, although one of the women had lost the contents of her stomach more than once.

After witnessing Lily Harvey's pregnancy, Lin suspected the woman of being in the family way. She intended to speak with her sometime soon. If she did carry a child, they would have to try to get some extra nutrition into her belly. A baby couldn't grow if its mother wasn't strong, and if she carried a child, it would be of Chinese descent. The first children born in this land were the tangible hope that their culture would survive despite traveling between continents. Those babies had to be nurtured, and tending children fell to all of them. Chinese society demanded that every member look after a little one as if it were their own, and that didn't end just because they were on the frontier.

She would find out about the woman sharing the space. Her cot was close to the stove, while Mei and Lin had found spaces farther away. Maybe tomorrow she would try to sit beside the woman and find an opening to discuss her situation. In any event, she would try to do so.

Mei sat cross-legged at the foot of the bed. Her legs tucked up and her head bowed to the sewing she held, she looked like a much younger woman. It wasn't until she raised her eyes and met Lin's gaze that the weariness showed. Hard circumstances aged a woman, and they hung like added years in her expression.

"You look like you're holding up part of the Great Wall with your shoulders, Lin." Mei offered a smile. It smoothed out the worry lines on her forehead and made her look younger. Not by much, but some. "Whatever is bothering you so much?"

They had become very close in a short time. While her new friend couldn't replace Violet, Lily, Pansy, or Daisy, she did make life much more tolerable. Enjoyable, even. That is, if Lin forgot that her heart had shattered when she left Wylder and Wei behind and that she lived and breathed in fear and apprehension about how she would get back to China.

Or even if she wanted to return to her homeland. As the days passed, the idea became less appealing. All she wanted lay behind her, and the sense of duty that propelled her forward had all but disappeared. Maybe she should have heeded Wei's words and accepted that her people were fine and would do well without her. They did not need a Jade Princess, and if her grandmother had sent her away, she must be certain that the province would survive in her absence.

How could she have been so foolish? She had tossed aside what really mattered, sacrificed a good life for a misguided notion. One woman could not save an entire people, and she had no proof they even needed saving!

Mei put her hand on Lin's arm. The touch, so gentle and reassuring, almost brought the thoughts tumbling through Lin's mind to her lips. She could share her distress and hope to find a solution in the sensible nature the other offered.

But no. It would not do to admit her stupidity.

"What is wrong, Lin? Now I am becoming worried."

She leaned closer and dropped her voice to a near whisper. "Are you unwell? Do you need me to find a doctor?"

A fast head shake to reassure her friend. "No, it's nothing like that. I am fine, really." But was she? Physically, yes. Emotionally? No, not even close to being okay. But that, like her admission of stupidity, had to be concealed. What would Mei think if she knew the truth? "I'm just tired, I guess." She spread her fingers wide and looked down at her hands. They were not as scratched as the other woman's were, but they had not fared well. One knuckle scabbed over and her fingertips were as stubbly as the bark of a cottonwood tree. She could probably clean dishes with them, no rag required. "I am not accustomed to manual labor, and it shows."

The other gave a tiny snort. "What shows is that you work harder than anyone else. Why, you're constantly dropping brooms into my barrel. And don't try to deny it—I've seen you do it. Not just once, but many times." She held up a hand between them. "I see you are about to protest, but I will not let you do so. Really, Lin, I have never seen anyone work as hard as you do. I don't know where you find all that energy. And I have watched you help others, as well." She tilted her head toward the woman in the bed nearest the stove. Her voice lowered again. "Her. I see you help her, too, even though you do not even know her name. Why do you do that?"

Why, indeed?

The truth came without thought. "Because she is one of us and needs help. When I do for one, I do for all. We all benefit from the collective good, don't we?"

For a moment, she thought her companion would cry. Unshed tears made the other's eyes shiny, and she watched as her friend swallowed twice. The silence grew between them, but finally Mei cleared her throat and offered a tiny smile.

"Yes, we do all benefit."

"Now I need to know, are you okay?" Lin placed her hand over the other woman's where it lay on the cot. The sewing had been forgotten, an untidy heap on the scratchy gray woolen blanket. "I did not mean to upset you. If I said something to offend, I am sorry."

Mei took her hand and gave a gentle squeeze. "No, you did not offend. In fact, you brought joy to my heart." She stopped and wiped a rough hand over her cheek. "My husband always said that, that we should do for others because we all reap the rewards of a good deed done. You reminded me of him, and I needed that." She swallowed again, then added, "It is good to remember those we have lost. It keeps them alive in this world, to tell their stories. And I think it must make them happy in their world, to hear us speaking fondly of them."

She thought about it for a moment. Rarely did she mention her grandparents, or even her brother. Perhaps she did them a disservice, trying to keep their names and stories from passing her lips. Maybe she should speak of them, breathe life into the memories she had of their time together.

"You are wise and beautiful, Mei. I agree, we need to speak of them." She took a deep breath and pushed herself to take a leap of faith. Confidences didn't come easily for her, but she believed she could trust Mei. She looked into the other's eyes, so deep, dark, and inviting, and spoke. "If you don't mind, I'd like to tell you about my grandmother."

****

One of Wei's biggest pet peeves involved wasting time. The hours and years allotted to them were precious and shouldn't, he believed, be squandered. Yet here they sat, waiting on a man who others said had information about a large gathering of women. Chinese women.

He stared at the glass on the scarred wooden table before him. He hadn't touched its rim to his lips and did not plan to do so. Neither the watery beer inside the glass nor the greasy thumbprint left near its edge by the last one who had used it appealed to him. Actually, both caused his gut to clench.

Why did it always seem that men called for meetings in saloons? Why not on the street, or in a reasonably civilized building? A diner, maybe. Or a bank. Or even on the platform of the nearest train depot.

Beneath a tree. Someplace simple, without raucous, drunken laughter or the irritating trill of women feigning interest in strange men in order to have them leave a few coins on their bedside tables come morning. Men getting drunk and women gaining the upper hand on male intoxication. And if the men left right after they satisfied themselves, which he knew most did so they could return to their preferred alcohol, the tittering would commence again as the woman rejoined the drinkers and looked for another who would pay her again for lying on a worn mattress and spreading her legs to him.

There were whorehouses in China. He'd been in one when he gained maturity. An uncle took him and selected a beautiful woman to initiate him into the arts of lovemaking. The event had been insightful, and he had been an enthusiastic student. As the gift had been paid for by his uncle, Wei did not have to leave funds for the woman. It had all been very civilized, the visit to lose his virginity.

It had been nothing like what surrounded them now. Here in the West, an establishment might be called a saloon, but any place that kept rooms above so its patrons could have sex with women employed by the so-called saloon was a whorehouse. It didn't matter that someone painted stars and flowers on a mule and called it a unicorn. Beneath the concealment, the animal would always be a mule. The same held true for saloons. Watering hole or house of ill repute? Just a matter of window dressing, to his way of thinking.

The other men didn't seem to mind their waiting in the barroom. Not even the Harvey brothers, who Wei considered to have moral and social values well above those of their peers. They each had a shot glass of whiskey, but neither had done more than sip the liquid.

He glanced at Thomas' face. The man watched a woman singing near the piano. She wore a low-cut red dress and dangling earrings, but he didn't think her appearance caught the man's eye. A look past the setting and circumstances, and especially the clothing she wore, showed a strong resemblance to the schoolteacher who waited for his return back in Wylder. The singer could have passed for Violet, or at the very least another Bloom sister.

Hard to believe that lives could be so different. Such a startling physical similarity, but the two women's existences couldn't be further apart. Respect, security, and a life that made others stop to share a few moments when she walks down the street. The other? A life so insecure she needed to sell her body to any man willing to pay, no respect from the community, and whispers as she goes about town. The disparity between schoolteacher and soiled dove seemed unfair, but fairness wasn't guaranteed anywhere in the world.

He turned to Thomas. "When do you think the man will show up? I don't want to waste the whole afternoon waiting for him." He hated that every minute squandered counted as one more that Lin could use to put added distance between them.

Harvey took his gaze from the singer. In his eyes, Wei saw that he pined for Miss Bloom. He wondered if the others saw him aching for Lin when they met his gaze.

"I don't know, but if you want to get going, we can head out." Thomas shrugged. He swept a palm across one cheek, filling the air with the rasp of stubble on skin. "Might be that he knows nothing we can use."

The man could be right. The fellow they waited on might not know a damn thing, and they might be wasting valuable time sitting in this dump.

On the other hand, he might be able to point them in the right direction, and they just might find Lin sooner than if they continued on their own without any clear idea where she went.

"Or he might know where Lin went." When Thomas nodded, he tipped his chin to the other man's whiskey. "We will wait a while longer. You need not hurry with your drink. No reason to upset your belly by downing it too fast and giving yourself an internal fire."

They both shot a look at the street beyond the batwing doors. An ominous, dark sky and cold breeze turned the picture menacing. No sign of snow, thankfully. Yet.

Thomas smiled. "I reckon an internal fire wouldn't be such a bad thing, now would it? But I've had one run-in with booze that changed my thinking on the subject, and I just ordered this more for the show of it than the whiskey." He nodded toward the grimy beer-filled glass. "As I suspect you've done."

"Yes, I thought that I should get a beer if I'm taking up space in the saloon."

"Good way to be, Wei. Respectful of another's livelihood and careful when in his place of business." The bartender barked an order for the woman to sing another song. The piano struck up a lively tune and she began again, while Thomas shook his head in unconcealed annoyance. "Yeah, good to respect a businessman of such a high moral character," he added. Sarcasm dripped from every word.

Time to change the subject before Thomas decided to put down the booze and stand up for the near-perfect match for his beloved Violet Bloom.

He offered a small grin and pointed to the whiskey. "It seems to me that I heard somewhere that you and Addison Merriweather had some kind of party. Then, you ended up at Miss Bloom's house, and…what? Something funny happened, didn't it?"

A snort as Thomas pushed the shot glass further from his hand. "A party for two, with a big dose of manly pity thrown in. Me and Addison, well, we were lamenting over women and the ways it's near impossible for men to understand what they're thinking most of the time. Or, why they do what they do."

He sure could understand that. "Hard to tell what goes through a woman's head. I certainly have no idea, and I, a trained doctor who should know what happens inside a person's head."

"Yeah, I know you were a medical doctor in China.

Well, if even you can't figure them out, there's no hope for the rest of us." The other man studied the amber liquid in his glass for a long moment. "No hope at all." He shook his head, then grinned. "And you're right, we did end up in Violet's yard. That is, after we drank way too much and got up a couple heads of steam over the injustice of being men with stubborn, impossible-to-understand women. It must be a Bloom family trait, muddling men's minds."

He had heard that both men were very drunk and managed to embarrass themselves in front of the women, including Lin. She had alluded to getting glimpses of skin she shouldn't have seen but would not elaborate.

"I heard you and Addison were a bit, how should we put it…"

Thomas gave a disgusted grunt. "Drunker than two skunks. And did you hear we behaved deplorably? Showed parts that no man should put on display when there are womenfolk around?"

He raised a brow. Now they were getting to the interesting part! If they had to waste precious time sitting around waiting for a man who might or mightn't show, they should at least tell some good stories to pass the time.

"I must confess, the one who told me the story only told part of it. She wouldn't, ah, elaborate on the tale, but from the way her cheeks turned pink I gathered there was more."

"Oh, Miss Lin had a right to be blushing over the memory." He took a deep breath, leaned close, and lowered his voice. "It was like this. We decided to go see Daisy and Violet and clear the misunderstandings we each had between them up. It would've been a good idea, if we weren't, as I said, drunk. But we were, and it didn't take long before we were standing beneath their windows with three sisters and your charming Lin staring down at us. Addison went down on one knee to propose, and his pants tore wide open, revealing his backside. And me? Not much good on holding that much liquid, I reckon. I stumbled over to the vegetable patch and proceeded to piss all over Violet's tomato plants."

Wei could not help himself. He laughed. And not a small chuckle, either, but a full-on, from-the-toes round of gut-aching laughter. No wonder Lin refused to tell him the rest! He could hardly imagine her witnessing the event, and knew she would never find words delicate enough to allow her to relay the tale.

"You didn't!"

Thomas sat back against the hard wooden chair. "Oh, but we did. Every bit of it, in all its undignified, disgraceful glory."

"Now I know why Lin wouldn't tell me the rest."

"Your Miss Lin is a good woman. And me and Addison, we pretty much disgraced ourselves in front of all four good women." He shook his head, closing his eyes for a few moments against the memory. "It's amazing that they were able to forgive us. Those women could never be faulted if they decided they never wanted to see us again. Fortunately for us, they are forgiving types."

"Very forgiving."

Thomas smirked. "Well, it didn't hurt none that it wasn't even a day or so later when we both came down with cholera. Nearly died, Addison did. Me, I just felt like dying. But Daisy and Violet, they stepped right up and took care of us. Nursed us real good. Then Daisy and

Addison got hitched, so all's well that ends well."

Wei held the Bloom sisters in high regard. But after hearing the tale, his respect for them increased. As a man of medicine, he saw the meaning behind putting one's own life to the back corner and tending to a patient who could put that very life at risk. It wasn't an easy thing to do, and anyone who willingly did so should be, in his mind, commended.

"So that is the lead up to the Merriweather marriage." He let the statement stand without adding to it.

As he knew he would, Thomas finished it off. "And hopefully, in time, I'll convince Violet to be my bride. Someday soon, I hope."

Since they were sharing confidences, he asked a question he'd wondered for some time. "Is Miss Violet opposed to marriage? Some people are, I think."

"Oh, no, not at all. We've spoken of it, but she wants to wait." Thomas' eyes took on a new glow. "She wants to be sure my daughter is beyond grieving for her own mama. Violet doesn't want her to think she's trying to take the place of my departed wife, is all. She's giving my girl time and space, at the expense of her own happiness."

Wei wasn't shocked. After all, Violet Bloom's integrity and compassion were on full view to all of Wylder every single day.

"She is a good woman." He paused and considered the way Thomas had mentioned time and space. The words reminded him of something he had learned in childhood. "Thomas, the way you describe your Violet as being thoughtful enough to offer time and space to your daughter brings back a very pleasant memory."

Thomas swept his palm over a spot on the table in front of him. He sat back in his chair, glanced toward the door, then said, "Please, tell me. It looks like we may be waiting a mite longer for the man to show, and I'm getting pretty tired of listening to that woman sing."

It had become clear that while she had a pleasant singing voice, the woman had a very small repertoire of songs at her disposal. She currently offered her third— or was it fourth?—rendition of an old standard.

"Chinese people have a few different thoughts on creation. How the world came to be, and how men began to walk the earth." He warmed to the topic, happy to be able to share something from his own land with his friend. "I was always taught about the great Pangu. He manifested from the infinite nothingness, the big emptiness that came before man. He arrived long before we were here, long before we began to measure time. Pangu came into being before the sky, the water, the earth. He came before everything."

When he paused, Thomas sat forward. It was clear that he wanted to know more, so Wei went on.

"Now, Pangu separated the nothingness into the earth and sky. The heavens and solid ground. He created the rivers and oceans by digging vast trenches and bottomless holes so the rain filled them with water. Mountains? He made those by piling enormous boulders on top of each other. Then, he crashed a fist on the ground to settle them into solid forms. He made it all for us." He spread his hands wide, and although they were in a dirty barroom, the embrace in his arms went far beyond the wooden walls. "Pangu made this for us, so that we can share time and space, so we can live our lives together. In harmony and with compassion, the way your

Miss Violet is doing. She is showing that to your daughter." He thought for a moment. "I think Pangu would be pleased."

Before he could continue, the wooden doors at the front of the saloon slapped open and Broderick, one of the men Sheriff Branch Wylder had sent with them to find Lin, walked through. Beside him, a man who looked like he'd been living rough for years. His blue jean trousers and jacket were stiffened by dirt and his hair hung in a long tail down his back. At his hips, a pair of revolvers—the only shiny part of the man's countenance.

Broderick tipped his head and raised a finger to point to where Wei and Thomas sat. "That's the man who wants to ask you questions."

Wei rose. When the pair came closer, he saw cold calculation in the man's dark eyes. Without saying a word, the newcomer made it known that he might have information, but it would be costly. He wasn't giving anything away for free. That was clear.

Chapter 6

*"Oh, my beautiful Little Jade Parrot, do not cry. We
are not made to be sad. Our ancestors separated the
earth and water for us, so that we might flourish and be
happy. The great ones did not build this world for us to
stumble and fall, but to laugh and dance. Remember that
always."*

Her grandmother's hair hung in a long thick braid
over one shoulder, and the emerald green nightdress she
wore sparkled. The queen brought magic with her. She
looked past the form bending over her where she lay in
her bed. Everything shimmered, aglow with a light that
pulsated with every breath she took.

She brought her gaze back to the face so dear to her.
The lines chiseled into the soft skin were ones she knew
well. The mouth pursed now, showing both love and
amusement. Care and concern, too.

A hand brushed across her cheeks confirmed the
gentle words. She had been crying. In her sleep,
apparently.

*"But Grandmother, there are sad times. They come,
even when we do not wish them. What then? How do I
refrain from crying when there is sadness? Longing for
my home? Missing those I love? I must cry for that!"*

A gentle shake of the wise woman's head sent the
braid whispering along her shoulder. Compassion shone
from her eyes, and her melodious voice softened. *"Oh,*

Jiang Ying Yue, you have a deep heart. A good, kind heart. One that is filled with caring for others, more than it is for you. But that needs to change, my little one. You need to worry about yourself. Take care of you, and let the rest of the world sort itself out. You cannot carry the weight of the world on your shoulders. It will not serve you, or anyone else, well."

"But—"

Someone shook Lin's shoulder so hard she forgot the words of protest she meant to offer the woman she loved so much. She scrunched her eyes tightly closed and tried to remember what she had been about to say.

Something about caring for others. For the good of all instead of a selfishness that would not be noble.

Another hard shake.

"Lin, wake up!" The voice wasn't the queen's. No soft, lilting speech or undulating words. No bright, glittery sparkles to accompany them. Only a fervent hushed demand. "Wake up, Lin. You must—I don't know what to do!"

Her eyes flew open. Mei leaned over her, her face inches away. Instinct made Lin press the back of her head against the mattress, but as soon as she caught the other woman's gaze she tilted sideways and sat. The thin blanket pooled around her hips, and a cold draft kissed her shoulders.

"What is it? What's wrong?"

She had been having such a nice dream, she hated to leave it behind, but the look in her friend's eyes left no room for doubt that she must wake.

"The woman at the end of the row. She is terribly sick. More so than ever." Mei ran a hand over her eyes and shook her head, as if it was almost too much for her to bear.

Lin got to her feet and hurried to the woman's cot. She did not look to be in distress. In fact, she was lying very still in the darkness. Almost too still…

She put a hand on the woman's cheek, then moved it so it hovered above the open mouth. A breath touched her skin, and the breath she had been holding released. Good. The woman lived, at least.

Mei stood beside her. They both leaned closer.

"She was crying when I went to wake you."

"She's not crying now." Whether asleep or passed out, no way to tell. But the woman lay on the narrow cot as still as a plank. It crossed Lin's mind that she might die at any second, but a good look at her chest showed the lady was alive. Not well, by the looks of things, but at least alive.

"No, but she's clammy. Did you feel her face? It shouldn't be so damp and cold."

Lin checked. Her friend was right. Something wasn't right. With child or not, no woman should have skin chilled and feeling as if she's recently taken a dip in an icy pool. She didn't know much about childbearing, but she knew enough to know this wasn't good.

"What should we do?" Mei's voice wobbled. "Her crying woke me, so pitiful and frightened, like a baby's. Only, it's her baby that is giving her fits, I think. Can we help her?"

"I hate to wake her. She's finally fallen asleep, and I would think that rest is what she needs." Food, as well. Now that they were close, it was almost painfully obvious that the woman didn't have much flesh on her bones. She glanced out the window to the night beyond. No way to tell how close they were to morning, but they couldn't be far. "Why don't we let her sleep? We can take turns watching over her, in case she wakes and needs help."

Mei nodded. Around them, gentle snores and the rustle of someone turning in their cot. "It seems wisest, to let her rest. I don't know what is going through her mind, but it is torturing her. I can't believe that a baby would make a woman so sorrowful." She sighed. "I wanted a baby so badly. We tried, but it didn't happen. And we thought we had all the time ahead of us, a whole lifetime, to try. We thought we would find happiness in this new land and make a family and home to be proud of. None of our dreams came true, and here I am, in this place without any hope for a good future."

Heartbreaking words, ones that cut right to Lin's soul. She had experienced absolute desolation and hopelessness after her brother was murdered. The morning Violet Bloom found her hiding in a cupboard in her classroom, she had been contemplating whether her life would be better if it ended, than if she continued to struggle to survive.

She would always be grateful that Violet found her. Took her in. Gave her love, support, and a new family.

"Don't speak like that, Mei." She whispered, so she wouldn't wake the sleeping woman they now stood over. The figure looked so fragile lying on the cot, a rush to protect washed over Lin. She would take the first watch and let her friend rest. Maybe it would give Mei a chance to shake the sadness that consumed her. "There is always room for hope. As long as we are alive, we should be hopeful. Better things are coming for both of us." She waved a hand over the cot. "For all three of us. She, too, deserves a future that includes safety and happiness.

Somehow, we will all get that." She turned and pulled her friend into a quick side hug. "Now, you go back to sleep. I will watch her."

"But you're tired, too. You need some rest."

"I'll get some. In a little bit I will wake you, and we will switch. But I'm fine now and don't mind sitting watch." She tipped her head toward the starlit sky beyond the wavy piece of glass in the window. "I'll watch the stars."

"Maybe you will see Fu Xing? We could use some of his attention, don't you agree?"

One of the star gods of happiness, Fu Xing bestowed joy and good fortune on those who looked to him for favor. There were others, but many viewed Fu Xing as the most powerful god of happiness in the stars.

"Oh, it would be fortunate indeed if he were to shine down some good tidings on us." Lin waved the other woman toward the far end of the narrow room. "Go, now, and I will watch. Rest well, my friend. Do not be afraid. We will all find our way to happiness again."

She watched the darkness consume Mei, listened to the creak when she climbed back into her cot. Then, near silence, the only sounds gentle breaths and an occasional soft snore. Her gaze dropped to the woman who she watched over. Still, sleeping stiffly. Whatever ailed her, whether it came from her mind or body—or both—it did not allow her to relax, not even in slumber.

Lin looked past the cots, and the women in them. She stared out at the stars and wondered if she had spoken the truth. Would she ever be able to find happiness again? She had known it in China. And with the Bloom sisters and especially her sweet Wei, she had been blessed again. But now? Who could tell if even the mighty Fu Xing could restore her heart and spirit to a happy state.

A big part of her doubted it. But then, as she had told Mei, one could not lose hope. Not even when the darkness seemed endless.

****

Wei had never been a violent man, but his fist curled of its own accord and a heat such as he'd never felt before filled him. He fought to control his anger, making himself pause before speaking. A most difficult endeavor, given that he wanted to scream.

Thomas and Theo both looked equally angry. Their eyes blazed, and with one on either side of him, they made a wall of fury. The solidarity brought only a small measure of comfort. Beneath it, the reality that they had just lost half of their search party.

Damn it. Just when it looked like they were getting closer to finding Lin, a fresh setback.

They had been delayed by weather coming out of Wylder. Thankfully, as the miles passed, the snow fell behind them, replaced by bone-freezing winds. Fatigue had sent them off course twice. Poor judgment when saddle weary made every trail look promising, even those that led away from where they should go. And the anger that came as a result of those misguided twists and turns made it all worse. A blinding windstorm woke them one morning, making it unsafe to continue. They waited that out, sheltering in a rocky outcropping for the better part of a day before taking to the trail again.

When they had to wait for the man to meet them in the saloon with whatever information he had about a large gathering of Chinese women working to manufacture some sort of household item, he had been impatient but saw the value in waiting. Hard to picture Lin making a product, but he didn't doubt her ability— not only to learn a new skill, but also to do whatever it took to reach a goal. And it turned out good that they had waited, even if it felt like they were sending precious time into the air, because the man who finally showed up in the saloon did have information. Hopefully, Lin had joined up with the work force and even now might be safely laboring alongside women in similar circumstances to her own.

And if she were doing that, staying in one safe place and trying to earn enough to let her move closer to boarding a ship bound for China, he had a chance to find her before she got to the shore. That came as his most pressing goal, to locate her in advance of her finding an outbound ship. If she did sail, his only option would be to find a ship and take the long arduous journey back to their homeland. Then he would need to travel great distances to find her before those she left China to escape did so. For all he knew, there were those still intent on killing the last surviving member of her dynasty, so they might claim the family power and fortune for themselves.

His blood boiled in his veins. A throbbing in his temples beat out a rhythm that matched the pounding in his chest. Every bit of him wanted to strike out, hurt someone—just to share the suffering. It did not make sense, he knew that, but sometimes logic ran off in the face of disappointment.

He did not trust himself to speak.

Thomas, Theo, and two of the men Branch Wylder sent to ride with them stood on a narrow wooden porch. He still didn't remember the men's names, but now it mattered less than ever. Fortunately, the rundown porch had an overhang, because a cold rain had come up. They were mostly sheltered in the small area just outside the doorway to a squat building in the center of the seen-better-days town where they had spent the night.

One of the locals had told them last night that a decade or so back the town had been a thriving mining community. There had been three active mines and the ore and gemstones pulled from the depths of the rock and soil had increased a number of men's fortunes. No one had gotten excessively wealthy, but many were comfortable enough to bring women to marry to the area, build good-sized homes, and open businesses. All had gone well until the mines dried up and the place went, like so many other newly sprung-up towns, nearly ghostlike. Many of the men who struck it rich took their money, wives, and families and went off for greener pastures. Lots of businesses failed, and the main street stood lined with buildings that had boarded-up storefronts.

Wei didn't regret that they had stopped here. After all, the man they had spoken with had given them a lead. A good one, too. Providing it panned out. And they could get there quickly. Life on the far frontier often changed as quickly as the weather. Sunshine to dust storm, all in the blink of an eye.

What he did regret—and it made him furious now—that they didn't leave town as soon as the man in the saloon had delivered and been paid for his information. If he had insisted they saddle up and head out, they wouldn't be standing on a rickety porch trying to keep from getting soaking wet.

And Broderick wouldn't be hollering inside the

doctor's shack. Wei had practiced medicine long enough to know that the size of the man didn't guarantee that it coincided with the pain he could tolerate. That is, the stature of a man didn't necessarily match his medical courage. He'd often seen men who were slight and small tolerate pain without flinching. And sometimes the bigger the man, the louder the scream, a sentiment that matched the sounds coming from the doctor's examining room.

His anger kept him from uttering a word, but he didn't feel one ounce of compassion for the man under the doctor's care. Wrong, he knew, especially since his medical training called upon him to be compassionate to all sentient beings, but in this case his feelings as a man pushed aside what he'd been taught in school. Because of stupidity, recklessness, carelessness, and a whole list of other unsavory things, they were diminished as a result of what happened.

Didn't people realize that one action had an effect on others?

"What the hell was he thinking, pulling a half-assed stunt like that?"

Theo's language drew his attention. They had been friends for quite some time, since Theo had moved to Wylder, and Wei had never heard him swear this way. A mild cuss word here and there, but nothing of this sort. Or spoken with such intensity, either.

One of the ranch hands pulled his hat from his head and bunched the brim between his fingertips. The look on his face echoed the anger in Theo's words. He wasn't happy, either. A glance at the last man showed they were all in accord on their feelings about their current situation.

"It weren't smart, I'll agree. But Broderick ain't never been good at refusin' a challenge."

The other man added, "Or a dare. 'Specially one that's got a coupla fingers of whiskey attached to its outcome." He shrugged. "Man can't say no to a free drink is all."

"Besides, it's not like he ain't never done it afore. That there man is legend at the ranch for divin' off a roof into a trough." He looked to his companion for agreement, and when he got it, he went on with a hint of pride in his voice. "Hell, that there man don't never miss, no matter how short or narrow a trough is. Why, he lands right inna middle, every single time."

"Well, he missed last night, didn't he?" Thomas' bootheels sounded like shots on the rickety wooden boards as he stomped toward the far end of the porch and looked out over the dismal scene. Barely daybreak, and already their plans were shot to hell.

"It weren't usual for him to miss." The man stopped mangling his hat brim and clapped it back on his head. "We was all surprised when he hit the dirt."

" 'Specially old Brodrick. He was extra surprised he didn't make it into that trough." The second man nodded, as if the shock of missing made the situation any better.

Wei's fingers curled even tighter, and it took all the effort he possessed to not scream his frustration. He reminded himself that he could not control others. He could only control himself, but at moments like these that, too, came as a near impossibility.

Theo snorted his disgust. "That man is going to be very surprised when he has to make the journey back to the ranch. The hollering he's doing now is nothing compared to what's to come, as you two drag his sorry ass across all the rutted trails we've traveled. Even if you can get him to a train station and haul yourselves onto a coach, it's going to be a miserable trip." He shook his head. "And I'm sure the sheriff isn't going to be pleased when he hears how his 'trusty men' let us down like this."

The first ranch hand got red in the face. "Now wait a minute, it weren't us that jumped off'n that saloon's roof!" He waved a hand toward the door, where a fresh round of moans could be heard. "Broderick had the idea all on his own to take that feller up on a dare. We weren't gonna get nothing outta the deal either way. No free drinks for us, nossir."

"But you didn't try to talk him out of it, did you?" Wei kept his tone neutral. He clamped down on the impulse to scream. To hit. To crash through the flimsy front door behind him and grab Broderick by the neck. "You watched while that jackass jumped off a roof and crashed onto a hard street beside a wooden box meant for watering jackasses."

The pair looked down at their boot tips. To their credit, neither attempted to put up a defense.

Maybe because there simply wasn't a defensible stance to offer, and everyone finally acknowledged it. Even silently, the truth settled in on all of them. Thomas returned from his place at the far end of the porch. They'd gone from a half-dozen to three in one leap.

"You should've tried to reason with the man. Branch Wylder isn't going to be happy when we get back to town and fill him in on this." Thomas turned and met Wei's gaze. "What now, Wei?"

There weren't any choices to be made. Not really. Whether he went with a big search party, or on his own, he would continue to look for Lin. Nothing would stop him—not even the foolishness of others.

He tugged on his hat brim and took a step toward the edge of the porch. As he stepped onto the packed red earth, he called over his shoulder. "We find her. Non-negotiable, finding her."

Their source had told of a large assemblage of Chinese women two towns over. A hard day's ride, or at most a day and a half, and he would be there. With any luck, Lin would be among the women, and he would be able to talk her into returning to Wylder with him.

The Harvey brothers followed as he strode toward the livery. He heard one of the ranch hands call after them, but he didn't turn or reply. They had chosen their path. Let them make the best of their situation, the way he planned to do with his.

****

Lin heard the whisper of hair sliding across the rough sheet and opened her eyes. Just before daybreak, from the tint of the purplish light coming through the window. She looked down at the cot, where the woman she had watched through the night stirred.

Since she took up her post and managed to rest a bit, she saw no need to switch positions with Mei. She let the other woman sleep uninterrupted and now, when she glanced over, saw her friend huddled beneath the thin blanket that covered her. She hadn't moved once.

The woman in the cot rolled onto her back, a hand coming to cover her abdomen as soon as she began to come awake. A protective gesture, one that touched Lin's heart.

All her life, she had dreamed of having a family of her own. A husband to love her, and for her to love in return. And children. Lots of them. So many that she would get out of breath calling them all to the dinner table.

The dream didn't look like it would become reality, no matter how desperate she was for it to become true. But for this woman, the one who had refused every offer of friendship and even now eyed her warily? She had a future family. No way to hide it. A woman did not protect an empty womb.

When she reached a hand to touch the other's cheek to check for fever, there wasn't any of the previous distance between them. The woman did not press back, away from the gesture. And when Lin's skin touched hers, she closed her eyes for an instant and took a soft breath, as if the touch somehow soothed her.

And it certainly calmed Lin. The skin was not clammy or hot. Whatever fever had possessed the woman during the night had obviously passed. Thankfully, it didn't look as if it had left any residual unfortunate effects. If anything, the patient's face glowed, and her eyes were clear and bright.

A deep brown, so beautiful and with an expression in them that begged for understanding.

It hit Lin that they had all been attempting to speak to the newest member of their sad little group in the language of this new-to-them land. Perhaps they had been going about things all wrong...

"How do you feel?" She spoke softly, so as not to disturb the others and used a common Chinese dialect in the hope the woman would understand.

"Much better, thank you." Her reply came with a smile. The Chinese syllables slipped off her tongue in a familiar cadence, bringing a warmth to Lin's heart. "And

I believe you are the one who cared for me, are you not? Thank you for that. It was a very long night."

"I was not the only one who watched over you." She tipped her head toward the far end of the room. "My friend is the one who heard you first. She came for me, and we both tended you during your unwell time. But you slept well, it seems. I am glad that you are improved."

When the woman tried to sit, she reached out and leant a strong hand. They positioned her against the bare wooden wall, and Lin pulled the thin blanket up high so that it covered as much as possible. No sense in catching a chill.

"I will thank her when she wakes." The woman met Lin's gaze and offered a tiny smile. "You have been kind to me before. I just…it's just that…"

"You do not understand English." She remembered when she didn't comprehend this new language. During her first months on the frontier, it had all sounded like magpies chirping. She managed to pick up a few basic words under her dear brother's tutelage and by listening to others, but it wasn't until she met Violet that she managed to become competent in both speaking and understanding English.

"I do not, no."

"It is isolating to not understand when people speak."

"You speak both languages with ease. I listen to you and the others. You are the most capable."

"I had a good teacher. It is not my doing, I assure you." She remembered the long hours spent with Violet, learning the English language. There were moments when she had been sure she would never be able to communicate well. But between her dear friend's belief in her ability and her own stubborn determination, she had mastered the challenge. If she could do it, anyone could. So she paused, then made an offer. "I can teach you if you would like to learn. If you plan to remain in this land, you will need skills. Speaking is a good one to have, and I am willing to help you."

The woman's distrust turned her dark eyes to pools of black. Her spine stiffened and she pursed her lips. When she finally spoke, the words were icy. "Why would you help me?"

"Why wouldn't I?"

"You don't even know me."

Lin had been taught to think before speaking, so she held her breath for a long moment and searched her mind for wisdom. She needed to convince this woman that despite their being in this strange land, there were those who could—and would, if given the chance—help her make her way toward the best life possible.

Her grandmother's voice appeared in her head.

Treat everyone as if they were a lotus flower.

The same flowers that grew in the palace gardens grew in the humblest ponds dotting the vast expanses of her homeland's countryside. And every flower emerged from its muddy home to offer beauty to whomever passed by, to all who appreciated its simple elegance.

No lotus grew more beautifully than the one beside it. They were all equal, valued for their subtle differences and worthy of admiration.

"I don't need to know you to appreciate you." When the other's brows lifted, she hurried to explain. "My grandmother had a pond in her garden. It grew the most beautiful lotus flowers. Pink, white, pink-and-white mixed…the flowers all rose up from the muddy bottom side by side. They floated happily on the still water, and as a child I loved to sit beside that pond with my grandmother and watch dragonflies dart from bloom to bloom."

Memories washed over her in a rush. Her heart warmed, sending a smooth, rich light from her center to every part of her. Right down to her toes and fingertips, she felt bathed in the beauty and memory of time spent with her favorite woman. When they were in the gardens, they were just them, no titles, no queen or princess…just Grandmother and her Little Jade. Of course, there had always been guards and staff in discreet corners and at distances close enough to assist if or when needed, but they were in constant attendance. So constant, actually, that they faded into the background.

Lin had the other woman's attention. She swept a look over the room. Everyone else still slumbered. The sky beyond the window glass had turned a brighter shade of deep purple. Time grew short for confidences.

And somehow, she knew that sharing a bit of her life, the one she had been forced to flee, with this person would not bring harm. Safety surrounded them, a secure cloak in the midst of an otherwise-challenging situation.

She leaned closer and lowered her voice a touch. "My grandmother taught me that lotus blossoms do not need to know each other to bloom happily together. There are no families, no lineages, nothing to separate one flower from another. They merely grow, float, and bring beauty beside each other. Happily, she said. They are all happy and supported in a pond." When the other woman smiled, she went on. "And they don't need to worry that one lotus will outshine the rest. They can be safe knowing that as long as they are all together, nestled in the pond, securely rooted in the mud and floating on the water, their lives will be good. They will have meaning. And purpose, and all because they each are valuable."

The woman dropped her gaze to her hands where they lay on the blanket. Lin looked down and saw they were as red and scratched as Mei's were. So she struggled with the broom-making task, as well.

She didn't speak, but waited for the other to pick up the conversation. Another thing she had learned at her grandmother's side, to offer space for others to feel safe enough to come forward and speak.

It seemed that nearly everything she knew came from her grandmother. So fortunate that the elder had willingly and kindly shared her wisdom. All her knowledge now carried Lin through everything that came her way, including finding a way to connect with a woman who clearly needed a supportive friend.

"I don't believe that we are all as valuable as we would like to be." The words were spoken so softly that Lin had to lean still closer to hear them. "To some, we have no value at all. Lotus blossoms that can be picked. Discarded. Trampled in the mud." She placed a hand over her abdomen. "To some, we are nothing."

She could have clutched Lin's heart with that hand, her words were so heartbreaking.

"Those who believe that are nothing to themselves. They are the nothing, and it is their own unhappiness that they push off on others." She put her hand over the other's and gave a gentle squeeze when she felt the cold skin. "You are something—you are someone of great importance. And your baby is, as well."

When their gazes met, she saw that she had been correct. The woman was with child.

"How do you know?"

Lin raised a shoulder, then let it drop. "You look like a woman who carries a beautiful secret." She took a deep breath, and added, "We all carry secrets of one kind or another, don't we?"

A brow shot up. "You have a secret, too?"

"Don't we all?" She ran a hand over her hair. The braid she had made last night before getting into her cot still hung almost as if it had just been plaited. Dozing upright had not disturbed it at all. "We each carry burdens we do not wish others to see. Maybe we fear judgment or ridicule, or even worry that we will be in danger if what we hide is discovered." She paused, then asked, "Do you fear for yourself? Or your baby? Is that why you are so secretive?"

If she objected to the questions, it did not show. The woman shook her head. "No. There is no one to hurt us, no one to care about us at all, really. The man who threw me aside has no interest in me or the child I carry. And the ones I came from Sichuan province with, my sister and our uncle, did not survive the ocean crossing. Many died on the ship. I will never forget the horror of that voyage…"

Sichuan province.

She came from Lin's province.

"I am sorry about your family. But did you say you are from Sichuan province?"

A nod. A shadow of longing passed over the woman's eyes. Lin could not tell if it came in memory of a sister and uncle or for the homeland they left behind.

"When did you arrive?" She didn't imagine it could

be that long ago. Most who arrived from China managed to pick up a few words in English, and this woman hadn't shown she knew anything much of the language.

"It has been three weeks. Two weeks at the coast, in a dark room near the pier that belonged to a woman I met when I got off the ship. She said I could stay with her family, but there wasn't a family in that horrible place. There were others like me, women and children with nowhere to go, no one to care how they fared after the voyage." She shrugged. "A few women were coming east, to the frontier towns, so I paid to be in the wagon with them. They went further on, but I became sick and got off here. The baby, you know." She rubbed her flat stomach. "I do not think she liked the bumpy wagon."

Three weeks.

Lin took the woman's hand again. For an instant, it was as if she held her grandmother's hand, a link to the land she loved and missed.

"How goes it in the province?" She swallowed hard, afraid to broach the question eating at her heart. "How are the people? Do they suffer greatly?"

A puzzled frown transformed the woman's soft features. Her brows knit, and she tilted her head to the side. "The province is doing well. Why would the people suffer?"

Not the answer she expected. But perhaps she hadn't made herself clear. "With the queen gone and the Jade Princess gone, how are the people doing well? How can they not be suffering without a leader in the palace to care for their well-being?"

"Oh, I understand now. You must have left the province before the new princess took our beloved queen's place."

"The new princess?" Now her own brows pulled together. She had no idea what had gone on since her departure, but it did not sound like anything near what she had been imagining. "Please, I am confused. What new princess? The Jade Princess came in succession to the queen, but she left the province before the queen..." Her throat tightened but she could not back down now. "Before the queen passed to the heavens. How is there a new princess?"

They were running out of time without others to hear their conversation. Outside, the sky had a bluish-lavender cast and was no longer dark. In the room, rustling sounds as women started to stir. Within minutes, someone would awaken and their private time would end.

Lin's heart pounded in her chest. A steady beat in her temples made her head start to ache, but not painfully. It was anticipatory excitement, which she struggled to control.

Dare she hope that someone had stepped into the role she thought only she could claim? Had another taken Grandmother's place?

A bolt of fear ran up her spine. Had the family who tried to murder her after killing her brother finally taken over the legacy that wasn't rightfully theirs? If they had, her departure for China must be top priority. She would need to get back as quickly as possible and oust the palace thief. Also, whoever else assisted in the wrongdoing would have to go.

"You must be away a long time not to know what happened after the queen died. It saddened everyone, her passing, especially since the younger Jade Princess was no longer in residence. The palace made it known that she and her brother had gone away, a command of the queen."

A command of the queen, indeed, Lin thought. If anyone knew how commanding her grandmother had been, they would be shocked that the genteel woman had such a backbone of steel and a will to match.

Now she asked, "But if the princess and the queen were both gone, who is the princess ruling our people?"

The other woman shot an eyebrow high on her forehead.

Lin realized her slip. *Our people.*

But the other did not point it out. She let it slide and went on with her explanation after taking a quick look at the room. Shapes were moving on cots, the light in the space grew with every passing second, and now murmurings broke the silence as women chatted.

"The queen had a sister. She is old, older than the queen, and has lived all her life in the mountains of our province. No one knew of her, not until just before the queen died. Then she summoned the sister's daughter, her niece, to the palace." A small smile tugged the corners of her lips high. "It was a beautiful and meaningful ceremony. The queen proclaimed the princess her successor. And since the new princess is not a direct descendent of the departed queen, the family that would claim control can no longer try to take any place at the palace." The smile grew and she leaned forward conspiratorially. "In fact, the new princess is not going to be a soft-handed ruler. No, she has already shown that the continuation of the queen's rule will be as forceful as if the queen still sat on the throne. The first thing the new princess did? She ordered the opposing family and their supporters taken to a remote compound in the mountains.

They work for the good of all and have no manner of escape. She has decreed that they will atone for the remainder of their lives for their attempts to steal the palace by serving those they wished to rule."

Lin released the air in her lungs. She hadn't realized she had been holding her breath, but it came as a huge relief when she began to breathe normally again.

The palace remained safe. The people who relied on a good, just ruler have one in place. And those who killed her brother and would have killed her, too, were sentenced to work for the people.

The queen had known all along what she would do once her natural successor had been removed from harm's way. Lin had no doubt at all that the matriarch had planned the entire event. It made it clear why Grandmother had been so insistent that her wishes be followed. She refused to deviate, no matter how Lin pleaded, and now she understood why her grandmother had been so steadfast.

And she appreciated her putting her own needs and wants secondary to the good of all. Lin knew in her heart that it hurt her grandmother to send her away, but she did it to keep both her granddaughter and the people who depended on her safe.

The other woman watched for her reaction, so Lin pushed aside nostalgic thoughts and smiled. "It sounds as if the people are well, the palace is in good order, and those who tried to do away with the province's rightful rulers are being punished. The queen certainly lived up to her lineage and leaves a beautiful legacy."

"She did. And she does." The other raised both brows in a silent question. "And some say that someday the Jade Princess may return to the palace. What are your thoughts on that?"

There were many, but none she would ever share with most people. Her beloved family had gone to great lengths to protect her and afford her the opportunity to have a happy, safe existence. She planned to carry out that way of thinking and honor the sacrifices made by the woman she held so dear.

Death did not ever fully separate those who loved deeply. She would always carry a part of her grandmother with her, and forever be her Little Jade Princess. But some things, like great love, were meant to be treasured and not put on display.

"My thoughts are unimportant. I am just a humble woman, in an unfamiliar land, with a new friend. And I do not even know your name." She smoothly changed the course of the conversation, deciding to ponder all she had learned later, when she found a moment to herself. "I am Sun Lin. And you are?"

"Happy to meet you, Lin. My name is Fu Ming, and I am very glad to finally make a friend in this new and harsh place."

Fu Ming.

So close to the name of one of the gods of happiness, the one she and Mei had spoken about just a short time ago. Fu Xing, god of happiness. Fu Ming, sweet mother-to-be.

It felt right that she should meet a woman named thusly. One who would deliver such important and unexpected news and who would, by its telling, bring a fresh opportunity for happiness to Lin's life. She decided then that they would be forever friends, she and Ming.

"Ming, do you have any other family? Was it only you, your sister, and your uncle?"

Sorrow touched the pretty face and Lin wished she hadn't inquired. But how could she know Ming if she did not ask about her life before this moment?

It almost seemed unfair since she wouldn't divulge the truth of her past. But that wasn't the same, she didn't think. To conceal her identity kept her alive and the palace intact. It had nothing to do with siblings or whether she traveled through the world alone.

"I do not. There were three of us, and now there is just me." She brushed a tear from an eye. "I am alone."

Lin pulled her into a gentle hug. She spoke into the other's hair. "No, you're not alone." She held Ming at arm's length and pinned her with her gaze. "You are part of a family now. There is me, to begin with. I will teach you to speak English. And I will help you with your baby when it comes."

"I don't know what to say…" Tears slid down Ming's cheeks. "But I don't understand what you mean by beginning with. Is that an expression that has a hidden meaning?"

Lin shook her head. English definitely wasn't easy to master, but she would be certain that her new friend had lots of help and practice. She would speak it someday soon and the hidden intricacies of the strange tongue would become natural to her in time.

"No hidden meaning." She took a deep breath and thought about her decision. It would impact both of them, and maybe Mei, as well, but there wasn't anything better in her mind. There wasn't any reason to continue on to China, and she certainly didn't want to remain at the broom factory. "I just mean that I have a family, an adopted kind of family. Sisters, and the men who they love, and children, even. I have people, and I need to get back to them. They will welcome you. They will become your people, too." She placed a hand over Ming's where it cradled her abdomen. Beneath their touch, a new life grew. "They will be your baby's people. A family for both of you."

Tears ran faster as the words gained meaning. Ming's face grew flushed, but not with fever as it had during the night, but with excitement. Disbelief, perhaps, mingled with joy.

They hugged tightly, and Lin's tears slid down her own cheeks. She had meant to watch over a sick woman while another who struggled rested. Her thought had been to care for those around her, and here she had been given a priceless gift for her trouble.

Had she ignored Mei and Ming, she would still be intent on going back to the province, back to the palace, to her old life.

Now, she would go back, but not to China. She would return to Wylder…and, hopefully, Wei's arms.

Chapter 7

Wei's anger had ebbed, much like the tide after a full moon. He often thought of the summers he had spent at the seashore with his family but had never realized how powerful a pull there could be when a force of nature exerted pressure. For him, Lin was the force. The moon and sun that made the blood flow in his veins, the shining star that kept him moving forward.

Anger for others and situations that could not be changed paled by comparison, fell off into nothingness. Left behind, renewed resolve.

They had ridden through the day and following night after they left Broderick and the others behind. At first, he had ridden like all the demons of hell were on his tail, driven by the furious heat of what had happened. But eventually his mind calmed, and he took pity on his horse. They had slowed but were not going slowly. Their pace kept the miles falling behind them, and with each one he breathed a little more.

Neither Thomas nor Theo voiced any words of opposition. They both settled in and rode steadily, as if they expected to keep this brisk pace. Wei appreciated their allegiance. He planned to show his gratitude when they returned to Wylder. He wasn't sure how, he could never repay them for the way they were undertaking this journey with him, but he would figure something out.

But first, to find Lin.

They had a discussion over their search tactics. A unanimous decision to stop in every single spot that showed human habitation going forward changed their plans a bit, but they all hoped it would pan out. The man who met them in the saloon said the large grouping of Chinese women gathered two towns away, but they reasoned they might miss finding Lin if they just kept riding past where she might be staying.

Now as they traveled, they checked in at every homestead, broken-down outpost, deserted-looking shack and hut. They even rode into a small settlement of natives who, while not being overly friendly, seemed to speak truthfully when they said they hadn't seen any Chinese women in the area.

Discouraging, to not find any whisper of the woman. But every day that they didn't stumble over a still female form by the side of the trail gave Wei hope that she would be found alive. He couldn't entertain any other sort of truth. She had to be well and alive, or he wouldn't be able to hold onto his mind. Or his heart.

"There's another homestead coming up." Thomas pointed to the building rising from the horizon. An hour or so away, if they kept this pace. "We can stop in there to ask. And maybe water the horses, too."

The animals had shown themselves to be just as loyal as the Harvey brothers. He wondered how he would show his gratitude to them when they got home. Perhaps a bit of specialty feed from the livery? He couldn't tell. All he knew was that everyone—man and beast—who helped him find Lin would earn his lifelong admiration.

"That sounds good." He leaned forward and ran a hand along the big chestnut's neck. The horse nickered in response but didn't slow its step. "They must be ready for a rest."

Theo spoke from where he rode on the other side of his brother. "I'm glad to hear you say that, Wei. I know we're intent on not wastin' time, but I think we could all use a short break to stretch our legs."

He had to agree. His own back felt as if it had been used as a railroad tie and weathered the abuse of a half-dozen fully loaded Union Pacific railcars. He had aches where he didn't think it possible for a man to ache, and blisters on his feet from keeping them in the stirrups for days on end.

A doctor first. Then, a gemstone dealer and jewelry maker. They had been his life's callings. None of those occupations required a man to travel for days on the back of an enormous animal through unpredictable weather in inhospitable territory. It all challenged him, but he would do anything to find the woman he could not live without.

Blisters be damned, he thought. *We'll water the horses, get the stiffness from our backs, then keep going.*

The sooner they found Lin, the better. Every day they were apart took its toll on him, and he wasn't sure how much more torture of not knowing of her safety he could take.

****

Voices buzzed in the workroom. A mixture of Chinese and English words married, carried by the confusion of the morning.

Women stood in small clusters, staring at the empty space before them.

Where there had been worktables, hard straight-backed chairs, and broom-making supplies the day before, now there were none of those things. A few wooden crates, a pile of broom handles, and some overturned baskets were all that remained.

No one knew what to do. They had come down from the sleeping room to work, but there wasn't any work to do. None that any could see, anyhow.

Lin looked over at Mei and Ming. The two had become instant friends, which made their trio very comfortable. She had hoped the other two would like each other, because in her mind they were already a small family. They must stick together, she thought, if they were to get to a better situation. And a baby would be born before too long. They must help Ming get settled somewhere safe before that happened.

So, it made her smile to see the two women getting to know each other so quickly.

Now if she could just figure out what had happened overnight. These past hours had brought so much of a whirlwind to her mind and heart, and a definite change to her plans, that making sense of one more thing, the confusing sight before her, made her knees wobbly.

She listened to the words around her. No one had any idea what had happened. And none of the women acted as if she wasn't shocked, so apparently this came as a surprise to all of them.

Ming and Mei stepped closer, as if they could draw strength from each other. She suspected their knees might be wobbly, too.

"What happened? Where did the owners go?" Mei raised her hands, palms up, and looked around. "No sign of either of them. How could they just leave us this way?"

"What will we do now?" Ming's eyes were huge. Lin saw fear in them, so she rushed to reassure their new friend.

"We will carry on." She reached out and put her hand on the other woman's shoulder. "Together. You, me, and Mei. We will stay together and decide what we will do next." When no one made a move to leave, she added, "Come, let us go upstairs and gather our things. There is no work here, so we will go."

The other two nodded their agreement and they turned toward the doorway. There was only one door and it served as both entrance and exit. She had often worried that if a fire broke out while they were making brooms, there would be little chance of everyone escaping alive. Now, the exit stood clear since the women were too stunned to move.

She led the way, but before she reached the doorway, two men appeared. One, the man who had hired her to make brooms, a smallish man with sharp features and bird-like eyes. Chinese, he had bragged that he had made large sums of silver and gold in this land. He promised that anyone who joined up with him would benefit greatly, as well. She hadn't any choice and no expectations of being showered with gold and silver, but he had appeared honest, and she and Mei needed to make some money, so they had agreed to work for him.

A large man came to the doorway behind him. Broad shoulders, coarse features, a scar along his browbone. He crossed his arms over a massive chest, straining the seams on his dirty brown vest. Unlike the man who had hired them, he did not enter the room. Instead, the big one stood in the doorway, a solid presence that effectively blocked the women in the work room.

The man who hired them did a quick head count. When he finished, he gave a satisfied nod.

"I see you are all here, and that is good. By now you see that we are moving to a different location."

Women's voices rose around them, but he cut the questions off with a wave of his hand. He raised his voice. "It is for your benefit that we move! This place is too small and we have found a bigger—a better—spot for this business. You will all be happy with the new arrangement, I assure you."

A shiver passed up Lin's spine. She didn't know how she knew, but she had no doubt that the man was lying. His genial smile and bland words concealed something.

She didn't care what he said. He couldn't convince her to go to another location. Between them, she and Mei had a tidy sum that would surely get three women on their way to Wylder. Time to speak up.

"I am sure your new building is lovely, but we will not be working for you anymore." Lin pasted a smile on her face. She, too, could be disingenuous. To allow the man to see she thought him a liar would not help them get away from him, so she added, "And the three of us"—she waved a hand to include Ming and Mei—"we wish you the best of luck with your new location."

When she went to exit, the man in the doorway sneered.

"Excuse me, please. We need to get our things."

She stared up at him, using her sternest, most businesslike authoritative expression, but he did not budge. Slowly, she turned to face the beady-eyed man. He stared at her with an amused grin on his pock-marked face. It sent acid churning in her gut, making her glad she hadn't eaten anything yet today.

"Please, ask him to move. We need to go retrieve

our things." She gave another smile. It didn't come easily, but she forced it. "Then we will be on our way."

The owner snorted. "You will not be going anywhere, except to the new location." He turned to speak to all the women. "And there is no need to get your things. We will gather them up and bring them to you. Not to worry, you are safe with us. And your belongings? They are safe, also."

Safe? Not one bit, she thought.

"You cannot make us go with you." It might not be wise to anger the man, but she would not just be carted off like so much baggage. Regardless of her location, she had been born a princess and refused to be treated with such indifference. "As I said, the three of us will collect our things and leave. Now, please ask your man to move from the doorway, so we can pass."

The man had the audacity to snort derisively a second time. Now, he angered her. How dare he be so rude?

"It seems you have forgotten our little agreement."

Agreement?

His eyes narrowed so they looked like tiny black beads set into a sea of wrinkles. "When you came here, you signed an agreement. You put your mark on the line and until you satisfy the terms of that agreement, you are mine."

"I did no such thing." She remembered that she and Mei had given their names and last addresses to the man. Nothing more. And the address she furnished was false, the way she suspected most of the others' were, as well. "I gave you my name."

"On a piece of paper that makes you mine until you satisfy the terms of our agreement." He waved a hand to the space around them. "You did not think these accommodations and meals were free, did you?"

"But you took that from my wages! You did that for all of us."

He shook his head. "I took some from your wages. Not the full amount. Until it is paid, you work for me." A gesture to the hulking figure in the doorway. "Now, you will all get into the wagon that is waiting outside. If you refuse, he will carry you out. And I promise you, he does not have a gentle touch."

****

Wei appreciated the hospitality shown by the homesteaders.

Two sons took care of their mounts, offering water and feed for their horses and some time in their small but clean stable. The men were invited indoors, an offer they accepted without hesitation.

The home afforded little luxury, but the wife kept it tidy. Homey touches were evidence that she spent long hours feathering their little nest with patchwork pillows and rag rugs.

With Wei, Thomas, and Theo in the small kitchen, there wasn't much room to move. The man whose table they surrounded insisted they sit, so they did. His wife, Honey, bustled about the stove making coffee and setting biscuits on a chipped white plate.

"Nice to see some fresh faces. Isn't it, Honey?" Tim Martin looked every bit the frontiersman, from his sturdy build and wide shoulders to the heavy leather boots covering his feet. His blue trousers were worn and patched in one spot but clean. His face had a sun-weathered toughness to it. Fine lines radiated from the corners of his eyes.

"It sure is." She set the coffee mugs and plate of corn biscuits on the table. "We don't get much in the way of company out here."

Wei took a swallow of coffee. Dark and strong, just the way he liked it. "Thank you for your hospitality. We're passing through, on our way to the next town."

"Yarnell's Corner."

He hadn't any idea what the place was called, but he nodded.

"That's right." He looked to each of the Harvey brothers to gauge their feelings on their hosts. Both men appeared relaxed. Theo's jaw worked on the bite of biscuit he had in his mouth. No sign that either thought they should be on guard. "We heard there is a group of women working there. Together, making household items." He paused, then added, "Chinese women. We've been told there is a group of Chinese women in the next town."

Both Honey and Tim nodded.

She spoke first. "Yes, that's right. They make brooms, I think it is." She shot a look at her husband, then met Wei's gaze. "I don't think it's an easy place for a woman to be. I mean, women talk. When I went to town last, I heard that the man who runs the place isn't a very nice person. He's…well, it's said he's hard on the women who make the brooms."

Wei's blood began to simmer. He'd gone from feeling relieved that perhaps they were close to locating Lin, to angered that women were being mistreated. There wouldn't be anywhere for the broom shop owner to hide if he had mistreated Lin. No place at all…

Tim put a hand on his wife's shoulder. Where he stood broad and tall, she presented a reed-thin figure.

Petite, with a mop of curly red hair that bounced on her shoulders when she spoke.

"Honey's right. I heard like talk from some of the men." He ran a slow fingertip along the blue cotton of his wife's dress. An unconscious movement, Wei was sure of it, but one that showed the relationship of the couple. A small pang of jealousy swept through him, but he let it pass. Someday soon, hopefully, he and Lin would have what Tim and Honey shared. "He takes the women in, keeps them locked in a room above the workroom. Doesn't let them out, and every so often he takes the group somewhere and leaves them. When he comes back to town, he starts building up a new crew of women to make the brooms."

Thomas put his coffee mug down. He'd swallowed more than half the liquid already. "A new crew? So you're saying he gathers women, delivers them somewhere, then comes back to do it again?"

"Yessir, that's exactly what I'm saying. We've all been watching it for a while now." He shrugged. "But we ain't got no sheriff out here, and no one wants to make any trouble with anyone else. We're all just trying to get by is all."

Wei understood that. In countless tiny towns across this sometimes barren and unforgiving land, people were just trying to do the same. Live and if not thrive, survive. Finding cause to bicker or worse with those nearby could spell disaster. Settling in inhospitable territory meant dealing not only with the geography and weather conditions, but with the bits of humanity that were either making the land their home or passing through.

"Seems like you're all aware of what's happening, and that's a good thing because you're able to hopefully help us find the woman we're looking for." Theo brushed crumbs from his fingertips and gave the lady of the house a smile. "And I do appreciate a flaky biscuit, ma'am. Don't tell my wife, but that was probably the best one I've eaten since I wore knee-length britches and lived in my mama's house. Thank you kindly."

Honey blushed. "Aw, my pleasure. I'm glad we could help you men out."

"You say you're looking for a woman? A Chinese woman?" Tim met Wei's gaze with eyes that were serious. "If she's been near here in the past few weeks, chances are you'll find her there. Seems they grab every Chinese woman who passes this way, and since the trail's one that heads to California and the coast as well as inland, closer to the rail lines, it's used a lot by foreigners." He paused, then added, "No disrespect intended."

"None taken." Wei swallowed the last of his coffee, placed his empty mug on the scarred wooden table, and stood. "Thank you both for helping us. And for your hospitality."

****

Lin's shoulders brushed Ming's on one side and Mei's on the other. Reassurance to feel her dear friends beside her, but also disconcerting to know they were all in a situation they never expected. One that did not offer an easy, immediate way to get away from.

They had been loaded along with the eleven other women into the back of a covered wagon. There were bench seats on either side, and they were seated facing each other. The wagon flap had been lowered, so they sat in semi-darkness. The air held a scent of something moldy and dusty, infused with the body odors of overheated frightened women.

In the far corner, one woman cried. She had buried her face in her hands the instant the wagon flap fell and had wept since they began moving. The woman beside her had patted her back a few times, but they were all lost in their own fears, and she did not seem able to do more. Lin could not blame her for her apathy. Every woman in the wagon had to fear for her life.

She did not believe for one minute that they were being taken to a new location to make brooms. As they exited the building, she saw the broom-making pails and supplies piled up against the side of a storage shed that leaned beside the building. They looked as if they had been tossed there, and if her hunch proved correct, the materials would be returned to the workroom now that they had all been forced from the building.

It wasn't clear what they had gotten themselves into, but it certainly wasn't good.

Ming sat furthest in the wagon, where the air smelled worse and offered not even the smallest movement. Lin worried the odors and heaviness would bring on a wave of sickness.

"How do you feel?" She reached for Ming's hand and gave a squeeze. It wasn't cold or sweaty, which reassured her. The woman felt physically fine, at least for now. "Are you feeling sick at all?"

Ming shook her head. "No, my belly does not protest. Not yet, anyway."

Mei stood and stepped around to help the other woman to her feet. "Here, change places with me. There isn't a lot of air that comes from outside, but if you push the flap over a little there should be a tiny bit. It will help you to stay feeling well."

When they had exchanged positions, Lin motioned for them to come closer. The sound of rumbling wheels, coupled with the low sobbing from the corner and the scattered opinions shared in frightened Chinese made for mind-numbing loudness.

"We need to get out of here." She did not wait for them to protest if in fact either had a mind to object. She didn't believe they would, so went on. "I would like to get us all out of this mess, but I can't count on the others to cooperate—not until we talk with them. Should we try? Ask and see if they are willing to try to break free of this horrible man?"

Both women nodded. Ming pushed the flap back a few inches and peeked out. "No one follows us. No horses behind the wagon, I mean. So if we get out, they are not waiting for us to try to escape."

Mei jutted a thumb toward the front of the wagon. "I think there are only the two of them. Up there. The big one driving and the mean one is with him." She scowled, turning her pretty features tough in the dimness. "I would like to smack that one myself. He told me that I was only giving my name so he would know how to address me when we spoke." She made a rude noise. "That pig."

Lin couldn't agree more about the man's being a swine, but now wasn't the time to discuss him. "So let's tell the others that as soon as we get a chance, we are all going to jump out. The wagon isn't moving that fast. I bet we can each drop out the back and help each other run away from the trail. There are scrubby bushes we can hide behind."

"We need to do it before we get too far from town." Mei passed a hand over her eyes. She took a big breath, and added, "We don't want to be out rough at night. It will be cold."

"And we have nothing," Ming said. "All of our things…"

Lin doubted they would see any of their belongings again. The man could not be trusted and had already proven himself to be devious.

"We have two choices. We can jump out closer to the place we just left, or closer to wherever they are taking us. I think that there will be other men at our destination, so we will be even more at a disadvantage." Lin weighed their options. They were few, and both were fraught with danger. But she could not be paralyzed by fear, so she put confidence she didn't feel into her voice. "We need to leave as quickly as possible. Pass it on to the others. Say we will help each other. Tell everyone to run back along the trail and into the scrubby growth beside the tracks. Don't go forward, go back—and help each other!"

She looked from Mei to Ming, taking each one's hand in one of her own. She gave them a gentle squeeze before she let them go and leaned forward to speak with the woman sitting across from them. Ming leaned close to the one directly across from her, and Mei turned to speak to the one beside her. One by one, heads nodded in understanding and agreement.

In the foul-smelling darkness, a sense of hope cut the gloom. They all looked to each other with purposeful gazes that hadn't been there before. Even the woman who had been sobbing quieted. Lin looked over and saw she rubbed her cheeks with shaky hands.

Good. Now wasn't the time for tears. Later, when they were free, they could shed happy tears, but until then they had to be strong.

Ming turned to her and pointed to the woman across from her, the one who sat beside the wagon flap on the opposite bench. "Should we go first? Together?"

Lin had counted. There were fourteen of them, so if they went out two by two they would only have to drop a total of seven times. Seven times to exit the wagon and run, and hope that the two men in front did not realize what they were doing.

She shook her head. There wasn't any way for her to know if any of the other women carried a child, but she thought it best if someone went before Ming in case the pregnant woman needed an extra hand.

"No, not you. I want either myself or Mei out before you, so we can help if you need us."

Before her new friend could say anything, Mei stood up and took a step toward the back. "I agree. I'll go first." She motioned to the woman seated on the end of the bench across from Ming. The other rose and nodded her understanding. "We will go first, then the rest of you just keep coming. I don't think we should linger, in case they discover what we are doing. And we will do better if we are all together."

Lin couldn't agree more. She looked to the others, and saw they were united in their determination to find freedom. A quick nod to Mei and the one standing beside her.

One deep breath, and the pair climbed over the edge of the wagon backboard. They held on to the canvas flap for a second, then jumped.

****

Wei pushed his horse harder. The animal already rode faster than any he'd been astride, but it still wasn't fast enough.

When he and the Harvey brothers arrived in Yarnell's Corner, they had no trouble finding the building where Chinese women were housed and where they worked. They also learned that the man who set them to their tasks had a reputation for being unkind. And the story Tim and Honey had shared, about the man removing the women from the building and replacing them with new ones he somehow found on their travels in the new land, wasn't unsubstantiated. Everyone they spoke with told similar tales, and with each telling, Wei's blood boiled hotter.

He had witnessed a lot of injustice in his lifetime, but it sounded as if the broom maker ran a scheme to supply Chinese females for a purpose that, in his mind, could not be honorable.

The man had to be stopped. And even if his precious Lin was not among the women the man currently housed, he would find out where the ones before her had been taken and look there.

That had been his plan when they rode into the shabby crossroads town.

But plans can get shot to hell. And in an instant, at that.

They learned they had just missed the current occupants of the broom-making operation. More than one person in town said the man had piled all the women, a dozen or so if they were correct, into a covered wagon and left town yesterday morning.

So that meant they had a day between them. One day, which wasn't ordinarily a huge span of time—that is, unless you were on the tail of a nefarious man in possession of a group of women, most of whom probably didn't even speak English.

Thankfully, neither Thomas nor Theo tried to slow him down. If they had, he would have told them to do whatever they needed to do. If they couldn't keep up, it wouldn't harm their friendship. But he needed to find those women and would not rest until he did.

From behind him, he heard Thomas shout.

"Wei! Hold up!"

He pulled up on the reins and slowed his horse. Hesitant to lose any time, he turned his head and shoulders. About ten feet back, both brothers had stopped and were looking at something lying at the side of the trail.

The horse took the distance in a few strides.

A boot. A woman's, most likely, from the size.

"It's a boot." He tried to keep the annoyance from his voice but didn't succeed. "We need to find the women, not footwear." When he started to turn the horse back, Theo held up a hand.

"But Wei, it's not dusty. It hasn't been here that long." Theo looked from the boot to the terrain around them. "Whoever lost it did so recently. That means that the woman is nearby."

"And where there's one woman…" Thomas let the words trail off.

"There may be more." Wei's eyes scanned the area beside the trail. Scrubby growth, cottonwoods in the distance, and a far-off mountainous outcropping. Desolate, for sure. Hospitable? Not so much.

Especially for a female, this part of the territory could be especially dangerous. Even if they were together, the women were probably unarmed. And unarmed females made for an easy—and enticing—target for both man and wild beast.

Even if the shoe wasn't Lin's, they had to look for the woman who lost it. The moral duty could not be ignored.

They got down from their saddles and searched the red dirt for signs. A strong wind had blown through last night, so much of the area had been scoured clean. When Theo called out, he and Thomas hurried to his side.

Wei knelt to look more closely at what the other man pointed to. Footprints. Many of them, leading into the scrub.

He stood and wiped a hand across the knee of his trousers. It certainly wasn't part of his plan to follow a trail off the rutted track, but they couldn't just ride away. None of the footprints looked big enough to belong to a man, so there were women who might need assistance. His conscience would never forgive him if he ignored this situation.

When he met the other men's gazes, he saw that theirs wouldn't, either.

They remounted and turned off into the scrub. Hopefully, the women weren't too far from the main trail.

****

Lin would never forgive herself if any of the women was hurt while they were hiking through the frontier searching for a way back that didn't include using the trail between Yarnell's Corner and whatever lay to the west. This had been her idea, to flee the wagon, and she accepted responsibility for the others. They had put their faith in her. She could not let them down.

It almost felt like a miracle that they had all managed to jump from the wagon undetected. When their turns came, none of the women hesitated, not even the one who had begun the trip in tears. They all jumped. Rolled a bit, some of them. And dashed for the scrub beside the trail. When everyone had made the jump, they ran into the brush and discussed their next move. Some had wanted to walk along the trail back to town, but most thought it unsafe. When the men learned they had lost the occupants of their wagon, surely they would return and search for the women.

They decided to walk parallel to the trail where they could. And when that wasn't an option due to an open stretch which didn't offer concealment, they walked deeper into the frontier. Now they trudged along silently, tired from walking and hungry from not eating for a full day. They had sheltered beneath some cottonwoods overnight but had not risked starting a fire, so they were chilled.

Lin looked at the others and considered trying to bolster their spirits. But what could she say, really? They all knew the town lay miles away, and no one had come up with a good plan for getting free of the man who held their agreement papers. Even if they hadn't understood what they were signing, they had all signed.

Ming sighed beside her, so she put an arm around the other woman and gave her a quick hug. "How are you doing? You must be exhausted, Ming."

"We are all tired. But for now, we are free." The run for freedom had loosened the woman's hair and now it hung in a glistening black sheet over her shoulder. With it out of its braid, her hair made the young woman appear still younger. Lin had wondered her age, but the time for such questions had not presented itself. Maybe another day, when they were warm and rested—and not fearful of being captured. "I am fine. And happy we are not in the back of that stinking wagon anymore."

Mei and the woman beside her murmured their agreement. No one missed the foul-smelling conveyance.

Or the two men who had forced them into it.

Mei waved toward Ming's uncovered foot. "I will gladly share my boot with you. Why won't you wear it for a while? Your foot must be aching by now."

They had all tried to get the woman to wear one of their boots, but she refused. Now, she shook her head again. "No, thank you. My foot is fine. It is my own stupidity that I did not realize I lost my boot when I jumped. My fear of capture blinded my senses. It will be fine. I am fine, really."

Lin opened her mouth to offer one of her own boots again, but the woman beside Mei cocked her head. Her eyes rounded, and she waved for them to stop walking.

When their footsteps no longer whispered against the red soil, they heard it. Horses. And if Lin guessed correctly, they were headed their way!

She motioned for the women to scatter. Mei and Ming joined hands, and the three of them ran to a boulder nestled in the scrubby brush nearby. They threw themselves onto the hard ground, flattening as much as possible. Lin's palm landed on a sharp piece of shale. The tender skin sliced but she swallowed the pain and did not call out.

The sounds of horse hooves grew louder. Their steps sent a trembling through the ground beneath her cheek. She prayed to Fu Xing, begging for his happiness to shine down on them all. They needed all the help they could get in such a frightening moment.

She didn't think the men—because surely the sound

indicated there was more than one horse—were the ones who had tried to take them hostage. They were with a wagon, and the horses they used to pull it didn't seem the kind to take to riders. They were work horses, used to move wagons and heavy loads.

Still, they were not alone in the wilderness. No way to know who could be passing by, and they could not afford to trust anyone.

Lin held her breath and intensified her silent pleas to the great Fu Xing. For good measure, she added in every other Chinese good-fortune god she could think of, listing them all in her head to keep her still while the danger hopefully passed.

In addition to the hoofbeats, she heard voices. Men, talking with each other from horseback. Their words carried.

"I don't see them." The voice spoke loudly, a deep, clear sound that didn't sound at all like the Chinese man who they ran from. "But there are footprints, so they must have come this way."

A second voice replied. "And the boot. Don't forget, we found the boot and the foot that went in it wasn't big. It's got to be a woman." The man sounded as cultured as the first one had. Again, nothing like either of the men who forced them all into their smelly covered wagon.

"A woman could not get far without a shoe in this terrain. Her foot will be cut to pieces if we don't find her soon."

A prickly sensation swept up Lin's spine.

Surely, she must be dreaming.

"I agree." The first man who had spoken replied. So, there were at least three of them. And they were searching for Ming! "We need to find the woman who is out here and get her back to town."

"And if we don't find her soon, we will be following a trail of blood."

She knew that voice.

She knew it as well as she knew her own name. Better, even.

Lin pushed to her feet, but before she could take a step both Ming and Mei pulled her back down.

"What are you doing?" Mei hissed, covering her body with her own. Her face, inches away. So close Lin could feel her hot breath on her nose. "Stay down!"

She shoved the other woman off of her and rolled to her side.

Ming grabbed her wrist and squeezed. "No! Stay down!"

Lin wrestled her wrist from the other woman's grip and pushed to her feet. She leapt over Mei's prostrate form and ran out from behind the boulder. Three men on horseback were riding away, between the brush and stone outcroppings.

She waved her arms, which made no sense at all because they couldn't see her, but it came as her first instinct to draw attention to herself. Then, she yelled.

"Wait! Wait, wait, wait!" She ran toward the riders, hollering as she went.

They slowed. Turned. And the last one jumped from his saddle and ran to her.

Wei.

Her Wei.

He was here.

This wasn't a dream.

He was—

Wei's solid form met hers, and for an instant time

stopped. He wrapped his arms around her and pulled her close. His heart thumped wildly against her cheek as she pressed herself to him.

The tears she had held inside for so long fell freely now.

"Wei—"

"Lin. Oh, my Lin—"

"How did you find me?" She searched his gaze for anger, but there wasn't any hint that he was upset with her in the familiar and oh, so desperately missed eyes. "How did you know I would be here?" She swept a hand out to the desolation surrounding them.

He stared into her eyes for what felt like forever. Then, he lowered his face and pressed his mouth to her lips. His hands slipped into the tangle of hair that had loosened from its braid, and he stepped so close there wasn't an inch between them. The kiss sent fireworks into her head and heart, and every question, every fear and discomfort, every misgiving she ever had about who she was and where she belonged disappeared.

She may have been born a Jade Princess, but in Wei's arms, she became a queen.

When he released her mouth, he wrapped his arms around her and pulled her against him again. His voice, close to her ear so only she could hear his words, had grown husky.

"I will always find you, Lin. Always." He stepped back and pinned her gaze with his. "And I will go wherever you want. You are my home, and I cannot stand to be separated from you again. Not ever. Do you understand?"

She couldn't reply. The tightening in her throat made speaking impossible, so she swallowed and nodded. A fresh wave of tears fell.

"I don't mean to interrupt, but..." Theo's voice cut through her thoughts. She scrubbed a hand over her face and met the man's gaze. He smiled so sweetly that she laughed out loud. "Now that's why we've been looking for you, to hear that pretty laugh, Miss Lin." He held up a boot. "Is this yours, by any chance?"

Lin turned to the outcropping to summon her friends but there wasn't any need. They already stood in full view. And the other women had also come out of hiding.

"Ming, your boot." She gestured to the man holding the piece of footwear. "It seems we may have been found because of your boot!"

Epilogue

January 1882

Lin looked up when she heard the front door open, then close. A cold wind blew beyond the cozy home, and even the quickest entrance allowed a slight breeze to come in and make the candles beside her chair sway.

The wind of contentment. Her grandmother's voice filled her mind, bringing the words that she had first heard as a child. The words she would soon pass to her own child.

Wei walked into the front parlor. He had divested himself of his hat, coat, and boots, but a light dusting of snow clung to the bottoms of his trouser legs. She did not care about such things. Let the man track water into the house. She counted it a blessing to have a home and a man and even a puddle to clean.

"I'm glad you're home. The wind sounds terrible out there." She accepted the kiss he planted on her cheek, and leaned back so he could rub a hand across her belly. The baby moved, as if sensing the loving touch. "Are Ming and the little one okay?"

Since they had brought the thirteen Chinese women back to Wylder with them, Wei had been helping Coyote with their medical services. The women were more comfortable with a doctor trained in traditional Chinese medicine.

And their arrival swelled the town a bit, besides. Thomas had financed a special business to help Chinese immigrants. He and Violet thought every person should speak the language of their new land, and be able to negotiate contracts without getting into situations such as the one the women had been entangled in.

Ming and Mei were in charge of the situation. Lin had helped much more early on, but now that Ming spoke English, she and Mei were capable of training the women who came to the big house Thomas had bought for them.

"Yes, she is fine. All the women are fine, and little Missy is doing better. She has a case of sniffles. I left some peppermint for tea and lemon salve to add warmth to her bathwater. A few days more and she will be back to normal."

Lin smiled as her husband settled in on the sofa beside her. She leaned her head on his shoulder and looked around. A fire crackled in the hearth in their little home. They had built this place right beside Violet's lavender house, so they could all stay close. That families remain together as much as possible had been a tenet of her childhood, and she wanted that for her own children, as well. Aunties and uncles nearby. Cousins to play with. A familiar face wherever they went, and always the knowledge that they had a loving, safe home.

She had never thought to find any of that for herself, yet here she sat.

"Normal is good," she sighed. "I wouldn't trade it for anything."

Wei leaned close and kissed her brow. "Nor would I. Ordinary days and a humble life. It's exactly what we all need." As he kissed her again, he chuckled. "Or as ordinary a life as one can find considering you're married to Wylder's Jade Princess."

Lin turned to nestle closer. She placed a fingertip over Wei's lips and smiled.

"Shh. That is our secret, my love."

She kissed him, then led him upstairs.

The snow could fall and the seasons could change, but Wylder was her home, now and forever. And that mattered more than any royal title ever could.

A word about the author...

Sarita Leone loves happy endings, in life and on the page.

This adventure-loving yoga teacher likes to travel, paint, and dance beneath the stars. She studies languages, enjoys making a mess in the kitchen, and never says "no" to fun. Finding pockets of peace everywhere she goes, this author plans to make every moment of this journey count.

Thank you for purchasing
this publication of The Wild Rose Press, Inc.

For questions or more information
contact us at
info@thewildrosepress.com.

The Wild Rose Press, Inc.
www.thewildrosepress.com